"Listen to me, Faith. Whatever I have to do, however I have to do it, I'll make certain you and Zoe are safe. I promise you that. I have a friend who can create new identities that Burke can never track. I promise."

"Really?"

He nodded.

She leaped at him and threw her arms around his neck in a grateful hug. He wrapped his arms around her, but within seconds, the warmth of her body tugged at him. Faith cleared her throat and stepped out of his arms.

He couldn't speak. His gaze fell to her lips and awareness sizzled between them.

She swallowed deeply and wet her lips.

He nearly groaned in response. He shouldn't feel this way. He couldn't. He'd already admitted to himself that however long it took, he'd see Faith and Zoe safe before he carried out his own plans.

Faith gripped his shirt. She blinked once, then twice and shook her head. "This can't happen," she whispered under her breath.

LAST STAND IN TEXAS

ROBIN PERINI

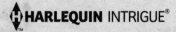

HARLEQUIN INTRIGUE®

This one's for all my Carder, Texas, Connections readers. Your letters and encouragement urged me to tell more CTC stories. This book wouldn't exist without you. Thank you for loving the Carder, Texas, world as much as I do.

ISBN-13: 978-1-335-60413-2

Last Stand in Texas

Copyright © 2018 by Robin L. Perini

Recycling programs for this product may not exist in your area.

Printed in U.S.A.

www.Harlequin.com

Award-winning author **Robin Perini**'s love of heart-stopping suspense and poignant romance, coupled with her adoration of high-tech weaponry and covert ops, encouraged her secret inner commando to take on the challenge of writing romantic suspense novels. Robin loves to interact with readers. You can catch her on her website, www.robinperini.com, and on several major social-networking sites, or write to her at PO Box 50472, Albuquerque, NM 87181-0472.

Books by Robin Perini

Harlequin Intrigue

Finding Her Son
Cowboy in the Crossfire
Christmas Conspiracy
Undercover Texas
The Cradle Conspiracy
Secret Obsession
Christmas Justice
San Antonio Secret
Cowboy's Secret Son
Last Stand in Texas

Visit the Author Profile page at Harlequin.com.

CAST OF CHARACTERS

Faith Thomas—When her Prince Charming turned into a frog, she struggled to provide a good life for herself and her daughter while dealing with her ex-husband and his powerful family. Until she discovers her ex's horrifying acts. Unable to trust anyone, including law enforcement, she's on the run to save her daughter's life, and her own.

Léon Royce—The most mysterious member of the elite group of operatives in Covert Technology Confidential, only a few know his true identity—for their safety as much as his own. When he chooses to protect Faith and Zoe, his cover is blown. Will his secrets cost all of them their lives?

Zoe Thomas—At seven years old, she hates this unexpected vacation because she's missing Little League baseball season, not to mention a trip to a big-league ball game with her father. She just wants to go home.

Burke Thomas—Faith's ex-husband wants custody of his daughter and will do anything to take her away from Faith. Even frame his ex-wife. But Burke's hiding a deadly secret behind his perfect mask, more lethal than anyone can imagine...especially for those closest to him.

Gerard Thomas—Burke's father has been grooming his only child to take over the family business. He's overlooked his son's spoiled behavior for years, even accepted his marriage to a woman less than worthy of joining their family. Can Gerard find a way to save his corporate empire from a scandal that could cost him everything?

Annie—The woman with no name, no past and only a camper to call home is nothing if not cautious when it comes to business. When Faith begs her for assistance, will Annie turn her away or help her disappear?

Catcher—This Newfoundland puppy could never have understood that he would put the young girl who loves him in mortal danger.

Prologue

The humidity weighing down the late spring breeze buffeted against Burke Thomas like an unwanted lover. At least the burning Texas sun would be at his back on his return to the civilized side of Dallas-Fort Worth.

The curtains from his ex-wife's dilapidated house shifted and she peeked out. At the sight of her, an exploding ache burst at the base of his skull. If killing Faith were a viable option, his life would markedly improve. He wanted nothing more than to break through the front door and give in to his desire.

Instead, he bit the inside of his cheek to rein in the unfeasible need.

Burke forced himself to take a slow, deep breath before turning on his heel and striding calmly to his Mercedes. He could maintain control. He *was* in control.

He opened the car door, but the new-car smell didn't possess the crisp, clean scent he savored. He peered down at the seat. A small streak of mud marred the leather.

Zoe.

His nails bit into his palm, piercing the skin.

Dirt from his daughter's jeans had soiled his car.

Unacceptable. His child needed etiquette lessons. Now. If it wasn't too late already.

He removed a plastic bag from the glove compartment and pulled out a clean rag and leather conditioner. Carefully, he swiped the mud away. His movements grew frantic, back and forth, back and forth, back and forth. The shine would reappear. It had to.

Zoe. Zoe. Zoe. Zoe.

With each swipe his daughter's name circled in his mind. He had to get control of her. If he could instill appropriate behavior in her as a seven-year-old, perhaps she wouldn't take after her mother. He'd come to the obvious conclusion that delayed training had been the problem with his ex-wife. Before he'd fully molded her, she'd ruined everything and forced him to divorce her.

After one last, vicious swipe, he studied the glistening surface. It would do.

He slid into the Mercedes and with a quick turn of his key, the engine roared to life. He glared at the now-closed curtains and screeched away from the house.

No more delays. He tapped his phone.

"Mr. Thomas?" his lawyer answered.

"Deliver the document. Now."

"It's Friday night after five. Our couriers have left for the evening. We can accommodate you first thing Monday."

"Tonight. Within the hour. Or do you want me to take my family's business elsewhere?"

Burke smiled. He could almost hear the man choke through the phone.

"Of course not, sir. The revised custody agreement will be in your ex-wife's hands within the hour."

"See that it is."

With a curse, he threw his phone across the seat, the frustration hammering his skull. His skin itched as if a rash bristled just beneath the surface. It was happening again. It always happened when Faith defied him.

Burke needed relief.

Sweat popped against his brow. He gripped the steering wheel. The familiar urge rose through his spine and into his head. The need settled and expanded, impatient and undeniable.

Why not celebrate Faith's latest punishment with his own personal gift to himself? Hadn't he denied himself enough tonight?

Burke jerked the steering wheel and guided his vehicle straight to the ideal hunting ground. He needed a woman.

With each passing stoplight, his skin prickled in ever-escalating anticipation. More often than not, he relished foreplay more than the act itself.

Tonight would be memorable. For both of them.

The search wasn't quick or easy, but Burke possessed remarkable patience. After two hours, his entire body brimmed with eagerness. He opened the car's passenger door for his choice, rounded the vehicle and joined her in the front seat.

Burke flipped on the air conditioner and sent his guest a sidelong glance. She was perfect for his plans tonight. Her eyes, in particular, had caught his attention. Big, emerald-green and noteworthy. Plus, she possessed the lithe figure Faith had lost the moment she'd gotten pregnant.

The woman's blond hair was just the right color, as well. It probably wasn't real, but he could live with one flaw. Besides, the dye job wasn't half-bad.

Either way, she would do nicely; she'd give him exactly what he needed.

She settled against the upholstery seat cover with a sigh and shot him a come-hither look. What was her name again? Randi, Brandi, Candi? It didn't matter. He'd just call her *sweetheart*.

He ran his hand through her long blond locks. She hadn't caked them up with hair spray like some women did. He let the silky strands slip through his fingers and bent his head to her ear. "It's too public to do what I want to do to you. How about a ride?"

"You got the money, I'm all yours," she said, her voice husky with need, her words slurred with intoxication.

His gaze scanned the road and surroundings. No police cars or cabs. He didn't worry about cameras. He knew exactly where they were located, and he'd paid well to disable those on his preferred route. He'd seen to the necessary detail the first time he'd used the Shiny Penny Bar as one of his selection zones. Tonight, all the vehicles were dark. No witnesses. He was safe.

She placed her hand on his leg. "Where are we going?"

"A midnight drive."

"How about a little preview?" She ran her fingers high on his thigh and sent him a flirtatious glance.

He gripped her arm to stop her from exploring too soon. "Not yet, sweetheart. I have big plans for you."

By the time they reached an elaborate garden park, Burke's heart pounded with anticipation. He pulled onto a side street and grabbed the prepacked supply kit from behind his seat. He held out his hand to her. "Come with me. I have something to show you."

He pulled her close, his arm pressing her rail-thin body against his. He led her to a locked gate and shimmied through the rails.

She grinned and slipped through after him. "You're so bad."

"I haven't even begun."

He wound his way through the English-style hedges to a small wall of trees. He pushed a branch aside. "After you, my dear."

She ducked through the lush oaks. He followed. They were enclosed in a small clearing, hidden from prying eyes.

"We're alone." She smiled and leaned against him, crushing her breasts into his chest.

"All alone," he whispered quietly, staring down at her, studying his choice.

The moon shone down from the break in the tree-tops. The gleaming light made her skin appear smooth and ageless, blurring her face so he could ignore the discrepancies with the woman who haunted his dreams.

Perhaps this one would quash the hunger inside of him.

He stroked her cheek with his thumb, across to the cleft in her chin. His heart kicked up a notch. The flaw proved she wasn't his dream lover. She wasn't even Faith.

His pulse raced, his breathing quickened. He should've been disappointed, but he wasn't. His body hardened with excitement of what was to come.

"What are you waiting for?" she whispered, nestling closer, grinding her hips against his.

"Almost," he whispered. He removed a plastic-lined sheet from his bag and spread it out, before guiding her a few steps to its center. His body tingled. "It's time."

She reached down to his zipper. He slapped her hands away, grabbed her hair and yanked, forcing her to look into his eyes.

She clutched at his hands. "Ow! What are you doing?"

With a smile, he tugged harder. Her eyes blurred with tears before the true nature of her predicament dawned on her less-than-Mensa intellect.

Burke smiled when fear, then panic widened her eyes.

He pulled a knife from the sheath at the small of his back and whipped the blade around. With joyful precision, he sliced long and deep across her throat. She clutched at her neck, but he knew his business. He'd studied. Diligently. For years.

She was dead in seconds.

Her body dropped to the ground. Her eyes stared sightless at the moon. He looked down at her and sighed. The cut had been deadly accurate, but life always left too soon. The efficient kill was a necessary sacrifice. He couldn't afford for her to resist too much. Scratching and fighting might result in evidence, something he refused to tolerate.

Burke knelt and tugged over his supply kit. He'd been looking forward to this one. The Eyeball Killer had fascinated him since the man's first mention during Burke's research.

He laid out his tools and studied her face. Green eyes were the rarest in the world. They would be a nice addition to his collection. He would have liked to collect brown, gray and blue, and maybe even hazel, as well. Too bad his discipline only allowed him the one opportunity to copy a unique modus operandi.

Discipline and preparation. That was what made him successful. And uncatchable. Regardless of his father's concerns.

Burke pushed her hair aside. Clutching the knife oh so slowly, he pressed the blade at the corner of one of her beautiful, blank and lifeless eyes.

Everything up to this moment had been foreplay.

Now for the main event.

THE MORNING LIGHT broke through the space between the kitchen curtains.

"Can I take the tablet Daddy gave me to school?" Zoe ran into the room at full speed and skidded to a stop in front of her mother, a huge smile on her face.

Faith folded the legal-sized paper and returned the custody agreement to the envelope for the umpteenth time. She rubbed the bridge of her nose to ease the building headache. She couldn't believe Burke had filed for full custody.

Undeniable proof she'd been a first-class fool. How many years had she believed she'd married Prince Charming, that he'd swept her out of the Shiny Penny, where she'd barely made enough to pay rent, and into a fairy tale? The only good to come of her marriage with Burke was her daughter. And the lesson Faith's mother had tried to teach her—never rely on anyone but yourself.

With a sigh, she gulped another swallow of coffee. She'd left Zoe with her neighbor half of Friday night hoping to find Burke, praying to talk some sense into him.

She'd finally located him near the bar where they'd first met, but not before he'd hooked up with another woman. Must've been some night, because he'd been incommunicado ever since.

Not that she cared. She'd stopped loving him long ago, but Zoe's well-being was at stake. Zoe irritated him more than anything. She couldn't imagine him taking care of her every day, seven days a week. He wanted a perfect china doll for a daughter. A child he could show off and then shoo away. Zoe would never be that. Faith's daughter was a tomboy through and through. She was messy, eager and independent. And definitely not a wallflower. Faith loved every inch of her.

She slid the rubber band off the morning paper. She'd have to fight the Thomas family machine to keep her daughter. To do that, Faith needed a job with more regular hours than her diner gig.

Intent on searching the classifieds, she spread the

paper out. Below the fold on the front page, a photo screamed out. A familiar-looking blond-haired woman smiled at her. The caption chilled Faith's soul.

"Local Woman Murdered. No Suspects."

Quickly, Faith scanned the story and stopped at a single paragraph. Mandy Jones's time of death was estimated between seven and ten.

Faith dropped the paper on the kitchen table, her body frozen in shock and disbelief. Faith had seen Mandy that night. She couldn't make herself believe this was possible, and yet, she knew what she'd witnessed.

Mandy Jones in the passenger seat of her ex-husband's car.

Chapter One

Three months later

The gray clouds threatening the West Texas sky earlier in the day had turned black. The air sizzled with electricity, and a rare drizzle of rain seeped into Stefan's skin. He peered at the sky. Strange, but the weather matched his mood today, so he'd go with it.

He ducked his head and darted up the Carder Texas Public Library's steps. Rain rolled off the brim of his Stetson, the incessant damp reminding him of the mountains of the tiny European country he'd once called home. A home on the other side of the globe. A home he hadn't visited in years. A homeland that believed he'd been assassinated along with his older brother during a failed coup d'état.

Instead, he was alive and well and impersonating a native Texan so convincingly he sometimes forgot he wasn't one.

"Hey, Léon, how's it going?"

"Can't complain." Stefan didn't blink at the use of his long-term alias. He tilted his hat in acknowledgment as the deputy limped past the library. Smithson had almost died a few years ago. Now he and his wife had a couple of kids and the guy never stopped smiling.

Something Stefan could never see happening for himself.

He couldn't afford connections or family. Which was why last night he'd made one of the toughest decisions of his life.

Stefan tapped his Stetson to remove the water and pushed through the double doors of the library.

A small girl sat at the front desk. A too-big baseball cap cocked to one side on her head. Her light brown hair fell halfway down her back. She looked up at him and smiled. "May I help you?"

He really should ignore her, or scare her with a terrifying frown, but instead he walked over to the desk. "Just browsing. Worked here long?"

"Do you have a library card?" she asked in a very professional tone. "You can't check out a book without a library card. My mom told me that."

Stefan fought back a smile at the girl's confident antics. "Nope. I like to read here."

"I don't have one, either." She leaned forward. "It's a secret."

He bent down so he could make out her whispered words. "I'll keep your secret."

"You're funny. I like you." She grinned up at him.

"Zoe." An urgent whisper sounded from his left.

"Uh-oh." The little girl bit her lip. "That's my mom. I'm not s'posed to be up here."

A woman hurried over, an adult version of the imp

in front of him. However, instead of Zoe's charm, she wore an expression that froze him.

He recognized the look. Not apologetic, not angry, not worried. Panic laced her eyes and had tightened her mouth.

Stefan took a step back from Zoe, putting space between them.

Zoe's mother scooted between her daughter and Stefan in mama-bear mode. "I'm sorry if she bothered you."

"Zoe was very helpful," he said with a wink at the little girl. "I definitely need to get a library card."

"See, Mom." She straightened her shoulders. "I told you I could help."

Her mother closed her eyes for a moment and pinched the bridge of her nose. "Do you need any assistance?" she asked him, entire body taut, practically begging him to refuse.

If he had any sense, he'd walk away right now. Most women would have smiled at him with warm eyes, but she did the opposite.

Retreat would be the best option. These two weren't any of his business, but something made him hesitate. Should he break his own rules, just this once? They looked like they could use someone in their corner.

The grip on his hat tightened. He couldn't believe he was even considering the idea.

"I'm browsing for now. I expect I'll see you around." With a quick nod at Zoe, he headed to the fiction aisles, keeping the pair in his peripheral vision.

As soon as he'd turned away, Zoe's mother ushered the little girl toward the back of the library.

Interesting. The sleeves of the woman's shirt showed a bit of fraying. Her shoes were scuffed. He recognized the Magic Marker polishing up the toe, but she colored her hair. The brown was almost too perfect. She'd fastened her locks away from her face with a clip, the strands hanging long and silky and infinitely touchable down her back, but with a slightly uneven edge, as if she'd cut it herself. Her gold-colored small hoop earrings might have appeared real at one time, but the tinge of green peeking through revealed the truth.

Her gaze had darted back and forth, hyperaware of her surroundings. He'd like to have seen her smile. He'd bet her eyes would light up just like her daughter's.

Stefan caught himself in his poetic musings. Okay, so she was attractive. Very attractive. Her body filled out her jeans very nicely with just enough curve to make a man notice twice. And he had. He'd also bet she was on the run and low on cash.

His curiosity—and interest—aroused, he worked his way down the book stacks. He could use a bit of intel, and he knew just who to ask. After he completed his primary task.

He scanned the sea of authors' names and even flipped through a couple of books. Surely one of the monikers would appeal.

A new identity came with a new name.

He'd be relieved to get rid of Léon Royce. He'd never liked it, but he'd been almost dead when it had been decided so he'd made the best of it. In some ways he already regretted this decision, but he didn't have a choice.

If he were honest, at first, he'd loved the CTC job: danger, excitement, helping people no one else could help. But ever since the Jennings fiasco, he'd volunteered for every dangerous, out-of-the-way job that CTC could throw at him, praying the next challenge would reignite a spark. Something inside of him had broken when that family had died.

Truth was, he should've left sooner. Would have, if not for the connections he'd made at Covert Technology Confidential. Except those relationships that kept him here also made him vulnerable.

He needed a new start, a new life, which made his curiosity about Zoe and her mother all the more odd.

Stefan wandered the stacks and each time he rounded the south end, his gaze veered to the woman. Definitely an upgrade from the middle-aged, sour-faced library assistant who'd stalked him when he'd visited several months ago.

The sound of creaking footsteps stiffened his spine before he recognized the rhythm of the familiar gait of the head librarian.

"Léon. You're back. I haven't seen you all summer," a familiar voice said.

He faced her and feigned surprise. "Mrs. Hargraves, how do you sneak up on me in those boots?"

Not that she really had, but they both played the game. Still, she'd realized he'd been gone for months, which meant she'd been watching for him. His behavior had become too predictable. Another sign he should move on.

Mrs. Hargraves smiled, a beam of pleasure in her eyes at his compliment. "Practice. If I'm going to avoid wearing quiet, ugly librarian shoes, I'd better be able to walk this place without making a sound."

She could probably sneak up on 99 percent of the clientele, too. According to Carder legend, Mrs. Hargraves had been the librarian since the 1960s. Dressed in jeans, Ropers and a flannel shirt, she sure didn't dress or act like any librarian he'd known, but the woman knew her books.

Over the last couple years, he'd let her pick out one book for him whenever he visited. She rarely went wrong. His favorite to date was *Inherit the Stars* by James P. Hogan.

"I've been saving this for you," she said, handing him *The Prince* by Machiavelli.

He nearly choked. He jerked his chin to meet her gaze. Did she know? Or did she think he needed lessons in being authoritative? Either one made the back of his neck itch.

"Thanks." He took the book, forcing a smile.

"I can see there's something wrong." She frowned at him. "Are you okay after your…trip? Not like that last one, I hope."

Okay, so she was observant, too.

"Or…" She paused for a moment and glanced behind her. "Is it my new assistant you're interested in?"

A small sense of relief loosened his neck muscles.

So his favorite octogenarian had matchmaking on her mind.

He returned the book to the shelf. "You caught me. I *may* have noticed both of your new helpers."

Mrs. Hargraves rocked back on the heels of her boots. "The last one quit and Faith needed a job. I liked the look of her. Been here a couple of months. She's always on time, she's no trouble, and that girl of hers is a pistol. Reminds me of myself when I was a youngster."

Faith. Her name suited her.

"You're collecting strays."

"Maybe." She crooked her finger at him, and he bent closer. "Faith's in big trouble. Skittish as a new-born colt. I don't know what kind of problem, but I get the feeling whatever she's running from is about to come to a head. You could help her." She narrowed her gaze. "I have a strong suspicion of what you folks do out at that ranch."

He didn't respond. "Thanks for everything." He kissed her cheek and started to walk away.

She grabbed his shirt. "She needs you. Don't ignore your gut."

Muffled whispers sounded from the tables at the back of the library. Stefan sent Mrs. Hargraves a subtle nod and followed the noise. He paused just out of their sight.

"What have I told you, Zoe? We can't draw attention to ourselves, and you promised you'd work on your reading."

"I *hate* reading. I'm bored. I want to go home and

play baseball with Danny. I can't miss the next season of Little League. He'll kill me."

"Look, Slugger, we need to stay here just a little longer. Then…"

"You keep saying that. I want to go home with Daddy. I know he doesn't like you, but he likes me. *He* wouldn't make me sit hours and hours and hours reading stupid books all the time. He'd buy me stuff to play with. Cool stuff." Zoe jerked away from her mother and plopped down at a table scattered with crayons, construction paper and children's books.

Ouch. Faith's daughter could strike a bull's-eye.

Faith stared at Zoe with tortured eyes. Stefan had seen it before. The heartache. The dejection. He didn't know exactly what was going on, but they clearly needed help.

Seeing a woman that afraid of being found didn't sit well with him. They needed help. Help he could give. If he could convince them to trust him.

THE RAIN PELTED Carder with no signs of letting up anytime soon. A rainbow crossed the gray sky of the horizon, leading to nowhere. Faith stood in the doorway of the library and studied the expanse of dark clouds. They portended the future much more than the pink and blue and green. Rainbows were supposed to hold magic and hope. She'd lost count of the days since she'd believed in either.

Zoe still did, of course.

Faith attempted to cloak herself in optimism. Maybe their luck could change, but somehow she doubted it.

From the morning she'd realized what her ex-husband had done to her car breaking down in this middle-of-nowhere town, she and Zoe hadn't caught a break. She'd fought against the panic of being discovered every day. Sometimes she succeeded, but she'd been unsettled since the stranger had shown up at the library today. Something to do with how his gaze had pierced right through her, how he'd seemed to see too much and how Zoe couldn't stop talking about him.

She didn't know how long she waited before the rain finally tapered off. The library had closed an hour ago, but Faith couldn't afford for their clothes to get wet or dirty. She didn't have the money to go to the Laundromat twice in a week.

"Looks like it's letting up," Mrs. Hargraves said.

"Thanks for letting me stay." Faith shifted on her feet. She didn't like making small talk. It led to relationships, and relationships meant being noticed.

"I don't mind driving you home, honey."

"That's okay. I have to hit the store first. I'm out of your way."

"Nothing's out of the way in Carder."

Faith didn't respond. Mrs. Hargraves had hired her off the books. It was best no one knew where she lived, not even someone as seemingly honest as her boss. Faith had to be careful. If no one knew where she lived, she could relax enough to close her eyes at night. At least for a few hours. "Pack up, Zoe. We're going home."

Her daughter ran up to her with a frown. "It's not home, you know."

Before Faith could respond, her daughter rushed to the back of the library. Heat flushed her cheeks and she glanced at Mrs. Hargraves. "Sorry."

The librarian patted her arm. "Don't you worry about it. She's a good girl, just a little frustrated today. Rain'll do that. I couldn't ever live in Seattle or somewhere like that. I'd be in a bad mood all the time."

"Thank you." Faith met the older woman's gaze. She'd saved their lives. "For everything you've done."

"You've helped *me*, honey. I'm not getting any younger. Speaking of which, I'm telling you, if I had fifty years back, I'd be all over that man who took a shine to you today." She winked. "You know who I'm talking about."

Faith didn't pretend not to know. "He barely said a word to me."

"He was watching you all right."

"Watching me?" A chill froze Faith. "Why?"

"The fact that you're a very attractive woman might be the reason." Mrs. Hargraves arched a brow in disbelief. "Come on, Faith. I saw that look you gave him. Besides, Zoe certainly liked our Léon."

Léon. So her boss knew him. Faith relaxed a bit. Burke had no connection with Carder, so he wouldn't know Léon, either. She was being paranoid. Again. "I couldn't place his accent."

"If you find out, let me know. Every woman in town from seven to seventy would like the answer." Her boss chuckled. "That boy is easy on the eyes...and the ears."

Faith couldn't deny he was attractive. Tall, with a rugged square jaw, that sexy, unshaven look and piercing blue eyes. He could be the hero in a fairy tale, his dark hair highlighted with sun-kissed blond streaks. Except this stranger had a sad, lonely darkness in him, and that kind of need pegged him as a troublesome cloud, not a rainbow.

What struck her as odd, though, was how he'd taken Zoe's playacting as a librarian seriously. The girl had fallen in love with him after two minutes. Faith didn't blame her daughter. Faith wasn't dead either, but since she preferred staying alive, she had to stay as invisible as possible.

Besides, he seemed too good to be true, and she knew better than to believe all those trimmings. She hadn't seen the danger in Burke, and look what had happened. "If you say so."

"Of course I do, and so do you." Mrs. Hargraves took Faith's hand. "Look, I'll let you in on a secret. If you need help sometime, Léon is a man who knows what to do."

Faith bit her lip.

"Don't ask me for details. I don't have all the answers. I just know if I were in trouble, Carder is where I'd want to be. We take care of our own."

Chewing on that interesting tidbit, Faith grabbed the large tote that doubled as her purse and waited. Zoe took her time but eventually dragged her feet through the front door.

Faith took her daughter's hand.

"Be safe, honey," her boss called out.

Faith waved to the librarian and the woman locked

the door behind them. Zoe skipped along, jumping in a large puddle. Water splashed up her jeans.

"Stop it. You're getting your clothes dirty."

Zoe stilled and turned to her mother. "That's what Dad always says."

Faith's heart ripped in two. She knelt down in front of Zoe. "I'm sorry, Slugger. It's just… I'm trying to find us a new home, a place where we can be happy. I need money to do that and it's expensive to wash our clothes. When we get our own place, you can dirty up those jeans all you want. In fact, I'll roll in the mud with you."

Zoe didn't meet her gaze for a few moments and then peeked up. "You promise to roll in the mud with me?"

"Pinky swear." Faith held out her hand. Zoe grinned and linked little fingers.

"I won't jump anymore, then."

"Thanks, Slugger."

Luckily, the family grocery store, which also served as the feed store and gas station, was only a half mile down the road. She and Zoe ducked in and grabbed one of the five carts sitting just inside the door.

Faith pulled out her small calculator. She picked up a loaf of bread, on sale, thankfully, and looked over at the peanut butter. Full price. They could probably make do another week with what they had if she kept the coating thin. Maybe it would be on sale next week.

"Can we get some chips?" Zoe asked.

Faith bit her lip. She shouldn't. "Maybe a small one. We'll have to wait and see."

Zoe gave her a huge grin, and the sight caused Faith's heart to sink. Her little girl shouldn't be so excited to buy a small package of chips. She loved Zoe's enthusiasm, but her reaction made Faith feel like a failure as a mother.

Every day she asked herself if she'd made the right decision, and every night she recognized she'd had no choice but to leave. Not once she'd realized what Burke was. She couldn't risk losing custody to a serial killer.

She tapped the cost of the small bag of chips into the calculator and scanned her list. Was there anything she could take off?

A scuff sounded behind her. Faith straightened and turned around. No one there. She clutched her purse tighter, hoping to push down the foreboding that laced her every thought. She picked up a bag of beans on sale and placed them in the cart, then paused.

Another rustle fluttered at her back.

A prickle skittered down her spine. Zoe examined a box of cereal, making an enthusiastic attempt to whistle the jingle. Faith glanced behind to her left, then her right. The store was small, a quarter size of the grocery store she'd frequented at home. She should have a visual on everybody.

Gripping the cart's handle with white-knuckled fists, she prodded Zoe along and hurriedly maneuvered through the last two aisles, placing the final four items into the cart. Maybe the weather had impacted her more than she thought. Maybe the fact that she hadn't heard any updates from her fake ID supplier in weeks had rattled her. Or maybe it was the man Mrs. Hargraves had told her she could trust. Léon. He'd come out of nowhere. He'd shown too much interest in her and Zoe. What if he *did* work for Burke?

She had to trust her gut. "Come on, Zoe. We need to leave." Faith couldn't hide the urgency from her voice.

Zoe frowned at her mother. "What's wrong, Mom?"

"Nothing. It's getting late." She headed toward the checkout.

"It's still light outside," her daughter protested, hurrying beside her.

"It won't be for long and we have to walk home."

Zoe shifted her knapsack, heavy with all her treasures stored inside.

The checker smiled at them. "How's it going, Faith?"

"Fine. And you, Maureen?"

The woman grinned, her face open and joyful, something Faith envied. "Can't complain. My boy just graduated. He's headed for boot camp."

"Congratulations. I'm sure you'll miss him."

"Yep. They grow up fast. Enjoy this one while you can." Maureen nodded at Zoe.

"I will." Faith scooped up the two bags and glanced over her shoulder yet again. She couldn't shake the being-watched feeling.

She had truly become paranoid. She wasn't made for being on the run. She wanted a normal life back. She just prayed that would happen once she could afford to leave Carder.

The sun hung low in the sky when she and Zoe walked out of the store. They had a two-mile trek to the shack she'd rented.

She started out slow. Not many walked in this town. She didn't even see a bicycle. Carder, Texas, was ranch country. Pickups ruled the streets.

The sheriff's office loomed in front of her. She crossed away from it, telling herself that she was simply making her way to *her* side of the street. It had nothing to do with the fact that Burke and his family's political allies could very well have convinced someone to put out a warrant for her arrest. She just prayed dyeing her hair brown would fool everyone long enough for her to disappear.

Whatever Burke was thinking or doing, it hadn't made headlines in the *San Antonio Express-News*. Much less the Carder weekly paper.

That strange unease settled between her shoulder blades. Faith didn't believe in ESP, but if she did, her spidey sense was going crazy. She picked up the pace.

"Mom, you're going too fast. I'm tired."

Faith slowed and turned around. Her daughter had taken to dragging the pack behind her. "Hand me the knapsack, Slugger."

Zoe held it out with both hands.

Faith took it and nearly dropped the bag. She hadn't expected it to be so heavy. "What have you got in here?"

"The books you made me bring. Plus my baseball, my favorite games, chalk and my shiny stones for hopscotch." Zoe shrugged. "So I wouldn't have to read the whole time."

An incessant pounding pulsed behind Faith's eyes, but she shoved aside the pain. "I don't want to get caught in the rain, Zoe. Let's hurry. I bet you can't beat me home." She fought to form the smallest smile.

Her daughter took off, and Faith jogged behind her.

"Stop before crossing the street," Faith shouted.

Zoe glanced back and grinned. "You won't catch me!"

Even so, her daughter slowed down a bit. When they settled in a new place, she'd make sure she enrolled Zoe in softball or baseball or maybe even soccer. Her daughter needed a way to work off all that energy.

By the time they reached the two-room shack she called home, Faith panted and bent over to catch her breath.

Zoe waited outside the door, shifting from one foot to another.

Faith slipped her hand into her pocket and dug out the key. She pushed it into the lock and opened the door.

Zoe rushed in, whirled around and raced back at her mother, plowing into her. The shopping bags flew out of Faith's hands. Zoe's knapsack dropped like a stone.

"What—"

Zoe's face made Faith's heart drop. "Mom, some-one's been here."

Faith pushed her daughter behind her and peered inside the open door.

The sofa had been overturned; bookcases toppled. The few items they had left were spread on the floor.

Their place had been ransacked.

"Zoe, we need to leave. Now!"

THOMAS, INCORPORATED OCCUPIED the top three floors of the downtown Dallas office building. Oil made the fortune, but Burke's father had diversified. They were now in distribution, energy storage and financial institutions. If you lived or worked in Texas, you dealt with one of Thomas, Inc.'s companies or subsidiaries. The business would be his someday, and Burke had big plans for the future.

For now, the company's reach equated influence, and influence translated into power. It also meant when his father called, Burke had no choice but to appear. He inserted his executive key into the elevator panel and pressed the button to the penthouse. The elevator zoomed upward.

A finely tuned bell chimed and the doors opened. Burke exited and crossed the thick carpet, ignoring the latest administrative assistant. Bracing himself, he knocked on his father's office door.

"Enter."

Burke took a cleansing breath and stepped inside.

His father raised his head and frowned. "Shut the door."

The older Thomas didn't smile. This wasn't going to be fun, and Burke had a feeling he knew the subject of the latest lecture. He closed the door quietly, as was expected, and strode across the room. "You wanted to see me?"

"Are you over the latest *incident*? Have you regained control of your *urges*?"

"Yes, sir." He met his father's gaze. "You know,

it wouldn't hurt if you'd help me out a little with this Faith situation."

Gerard Thomas shot to his feet. "How dare you speak to me that way. Help you? I've saved you from going to prison more times than you'll ever know. It's only been two weeks since the previous *problem* occurred. Two weeks. Have you *no* discipline?"

Burke ground his nails into one palm. "I keep getting calls from investigators and lawyers. It's…frustrating. I need to relieve my…stress."

"Then go for a run. Lift some weights, but don't…" His father scowled and slugged a shot of whiskey. "Your mother wants to see Zoe. I'm running out of excuses."

"I'll visit Mom, make up something." Burke shrugged with indifference.

"You think this is a game?" His father slammed the glass onto his desk. "You're too impatient. You have no self-discipline. You should have waited until we nailed down the case against Faith before serving the proposed custody agreement."

"You're the one who told Mother we were ready." Burke lifted his chin. "How could I predict she'd run?"

"How many times have I told you to run any decision that affects this family by me first?" His father rubbed his eyes. "Faith might not be fit to raise my granddaughter, but neither are you. I needed an airtight case of neglect to ensure you get custody."

"Well, she's taken Zoe without my permission. That's a plus."

"*If* we find her."

"I can fix this," Burke said under his breath. "If you give me the leeway, when I find her—"

His father slammed his hand on the desk. "Do not even *think* about harming Faith."

Burke's lips pursed.

"The cost of cleaning up your messes just doubled. If my team hadn't gone in behind you, you would've been caught. Your DNA was there, Burke. You're getting sloppy.

"If you do something to your ex-wife, I won't be able to protect you, or our family name. My sway only goes so far." His father took a seat, steepled his fingers and stared over the tips at Burke. "Get control of yourself and get back to work."

The stinging words pierced Burke's skin with the force of icy knives, but he said nothing. He simply nodded and crossed the hall to his own office.

Once inside, he slammed his fist into the wall. How had his father found out about his latest indiscretion so fast?

His head pounded in a rhythmic crashing against his skull. He placed the heel of his hand against his temple. This was all Faith's fault. She was the one who'd taken Zoe, and because of it, his mother was a basket case. His father...

He didn't give a damn about Gerard Thomas or how he felt.

Burke rubbed his face. Faith had been gone three months. She wasn't smart enough to disappear completely. She would make a mistake. And then he'd have her. No matter what his father said.

He sagged into the leather chair behind his desk and tossed his phone onto the perfectly polished mahogany. He unlocked the top drawer and pulled out a folder containing his plans for the future. When *he* ran Thomas, Incorporated.

He flipped through the pages. Burke would expand the company's power nationally, and then internationally. There would be no limits.

His cell vibrated to life.

He glanced at the caller. Orren better have some good news. "Report."

"Mr. Thomas. We found her."

Chapter Two

Stefan's SUV bounced over the West Texas badlands, putting his back-road driving skills to the test. He glanced at his GPS. He should be there soon. A strip of vivid purple and orange winked at him from the western horizon, the only color except for a few blooming cacti. The harsh landscape didn't mince words; dramatic, beautiful in its own way, but nothing like his home country of Bellevaux, strewn with lakes and rivers, lush rolling green hills and vineyards.

His vehicle kicked up dust from the parched earth. He'd been traveling a cattle trail for a half hour, and he just hoped he'd picked the right path. He'd never rendezvoused with Annie in the same place twice. The woman put his own paranoia to shame.

On the other hand, she survived when by all rights she should be dead.

They both lived in the world of gray shadows, where light and dark, truth and lies, right and wrong fused into a strange, inseparable muddle.

The vehicle rose in elevation just enough to see another mile or so into the distance when he made out the top of a nondescript tow camper.

Right where she said she'd be.

He pulled his SUV about fifty feet from her make-shift home and exited, hands raised, leaving his SIG Sauer in the vehicle. Annie had her rules about guns, after all.

She didn't show herself, but he knew she could see him. Probably had her sight trained on him right now.

"Annie?" he called out.

She didn't answer, so he waited.

And waited.

A figure finally rose from the protection of a group of saltbushes. Annie cradled an Uzi, her favorite weapon, and strode toward him. She'd piled her loose curly hair on top of her head, not the dark brown he re-called from their first meeting or the auburn from their last appointment. No, this visit, golden brown kissed with blond framed her face, highlighting an unexpected softness to her appearance. Maybe her natural color. He couldn't be certain, but it suited her.

She wore her usual black jeans and a too-large black T-shirt. By the time the sun set she'd be practically in-visible.

Her smile widened when she reached him, a smile that revealed the hidden beauty she made an effort to conceal. He'd never understood why.

"Léon, you look good for a dead man."

"And you look too beautiful to be dead."

He bent down and kissed her cheek gently. They'd been friends for about five years now. She knew him as well as anybody, but even she didn't know his true identity. When CTC had smuggled him into the United States to save his life, they had provided her the information for his Léon Royce persona, but the company had never revealed his real name.

"How've you been, Annie?"

A shadowed expression he recognized all too well crossed her face. "Not bad. And you?"

Just the sort of conversation friends with benefits had when they kept each other at arm's length. Two people with major trust issues and on the run didn't make for a good long-term relationship. They'd recognized the reality early on, so they performed the identical dance each time they met.

"You planning on coming out of hiding anytime soon?" He always asked.

"Probably not. I just got my hair done for the apocalypse," she said with a sad smile. "You and I made our choices years ago. This is my life now—helping troublemakers like you and innocent people who have nowhere else to turn."

Faith and her daughter flashed into his mind. He shoved them aside. He really shouldn't care.

Except he did.

"So, business has been good?"

"Better than ever." She sighed. "Power corrupts everything. Law enforcement and government included. Sometimes disappearing is the only answer."

"Truer words."

"So why the smoke signal?" she asked. "Ransom usually contacts me for a job."

"This is personal." Stefan shifted his weight and met her gaze, direct and unwavering. "I need to disappear."

She let out a low whistle. "You're leaving CTC?"

He nodded.

"I see." She strode across her campsite and unlocked a series of padlocks she'd attached to the reinforced door of the camper. "Come inside."

He removed his hat and ducked inside. The last time she'd invited him in, they'd headed straight to the bedroom. This time he took the opposite turn to a sophisticated set of equipment, a high-tech wizard's dream. Annie could forge any identification card needed. She could backstop an elaborate past, or tap into satellite imagery and even street cameras—for a price. He didn't want to think about what other intel she could lay her hands on.

She slid behind her desk.

"Léon needs to die a public death," he said, sitting across from her. "I want a new identity. A fresh start. A clean slate."

She quirked an eyebrow. "Does Ransom know?"

"You're the first."

She smiled in that knowing way of hers. "Yeah, right. He knows something is up."

"Probably."

Her fingers flew across a keyboard. "I can kill Léon without too much trouble. Creating someone brand-new could take a bit longer. Are you at risk?"

Her forehead furrowed. He recognized the worry. "I'm not in imminent danger, but it's only a matter of time. I've gotten sloppy, made too many connections. It could be dangerous if—"

"The people wanting to kill you ever found you," she finished. "Why do you think I live out of a trailer? I can't afford long-term anything." Annie leaned back in her chair. "Starting over isn't all it's cracked up to be, either."

Like Faith was obviously trying to do. Her terrified expression suddenly came to mind. Helping people like her was what CTC did—and what Annie did. What *he* tried to do.

"I can't go back to who I was." He drummed his fingers on his leg. How could he put his desire into words that didn't sound ridiculous? "I want—"

"A normal life." Annie chuckled and he met her gaze. Despite her laughter, commiseration laced Annie's eyes. "The minute you chose to play spy guy, you hung up the normal hat."

"You have no idea how true that statement is." He'd become Léon Royce because of his undercover work. He'd become a ghost to his family and his country because of his own choices. Now, he had to live with the consequences.

She rounded her desk and hitched her hip on its edge. "I may not know your true identity, but I doubt you were ever ordinary. That's what you'll have to become for this to work."

Stefan flicked the brim of his Stetson. "Ordinary. I like the sound of that."

THE LITTLE SHACK they'd called home wasn't safe. Faith
nails bit into her palm, trying not to let Zoe see her true
panic. Her gaze raced through the room. Nothing had
been left untouched. Even the bookcase shelves had
been strewn across the floor. The coffee table lay on
its side. Faith's heart raced as she surveyed the damage. She couldn't move. She couldn't breathe.

She could only protect her daughter.

In her old life, she would've immediately rushed to a
neighbor's house and called the police. She didn't have
that luxury now. They were alone, and everything they
owned was inside that house. She couldn't walk away.

Faith stepped just inside the door and reached to
her left. Zoe's baseball bat was still propped in the
corner. She snagged it and curled her fingers around
the wooden neck.

"If you're still here, get out. I'm armed," she shouted.

No one answered. The shack was eerily quiet. She
circled and her gaze scanned every inch of their small,
furnished rental. Nothing had been left untouched.

There went her security deposit.

"Stay here," Faith whispered to Zoe. "If anyone
comes, run and hide in the trees behind the houses.
I'll find you."

Her daughter gripped her knapsack and nodded, her
small face terrified.

Clutching the bat with all her strength, Faith tiptoed into the small kitchenette. Everything had been
chucked out of the cupboards. What had they been
looking for? If it was money... Oh, God.

She rushed into the small bedroom. The mattresses

she and Zoe slept on had been tossed; their clothes were scattered across the floor.

Her gaze stopped at the closed closet door. The blood pounded against her temples. Slowly, carefully, she approached. Her fingers folded into the recessed handle and she yanked open the door.

The wood slid on the rails and rammed into the wall at the other end with a clatter.

Empty. No one was here.

She couldn't breathe yet.

After checking the bathroom and shower, Faith sank onto the bed. Now, she could breathe. "Come here, Zoe," she called. "It's safe."

The little girl ran in and leaped at her mother. Faith held her close and rocked her for a few moments. "We're okay. That's all that matters."

"Did they steal anything?" Zoe asked from her lap. "Did they take Rainbow?"

"Your unicorn? I don't think so."

"Where is she?"

Faith's gaze scanned the room. No stuffed toy. "Maybe under the bed?"

Zoe slipped out of Faith's arms and got down on her hands and knees. She peered under the rickety bed frame and squirmed underneath before popping out, holding the colorful animal.

"I got her. Rainbow was hiding from the bald man. She's smart that way."

At her daughter's words, Faith stilled. "Zoe, did you see someone?"

Her daughter shrugged.

"Zoe?"

"I saw a big man with a bald head follow us in the grocery store. Whenever you turned around, he hid. I thought he was playing a game."

Faith rubbed her eyes as the realization hit her. "Was he tall like Daddy?"

"Yes. With a mermaid drawing on his arm."

The tattoo. She'd seen the man before, but not in Carder. The more Faith racked her brain, the more her memories coalesced. In Weatherford. He'd been hired as the bouncer at the Shiny Penny about the time she began dating Burke. What were the odds that a man working at the bar would end up at a grocery store in Carder?

Only one person could be responsible for this happening.

Burke had found them.

They had to leave Carder. Now.

Knees trembling, Faith knelt beside the bed and shoved aside the nightstand. She pried up the carpet. An envelope was tucked beneath the poorly installed rug. Hands shaking, she pulled it out and fingered through the bills.

Her entire body sagged in relief. She plopped down in the middle of the bedroom, grasping the envelope, their lifeline, the money she'd raised to pay for the car repairs so they could leave Carder.

At one time, there had been two envelopes hidden here. In the first one, she'd placed all the money she'd scraped together from selling her wedding ring and all the jewelry her husband had given her. Most of which had been fake.

It hadn't been enough to pay for new identities for her and Zoe. Her contact had required $10,000 up front. To make up the difference, she'd been forced to sell the small diamond ring her mother had given her before her death.

The money represented their escape, their chance to get away from the past, and from Burke.

If he ever discovered that she knew what he'd done, he wouldn't just take Zoe from her. He'd kill her to keep his secret.

"Mom? Are you okay?"

Faith swiped at her eyes. "I'm fine. We're fine."

"Why are you crying?" Zoe hugged her unicorn, the vulnerable expression breaking Faith's heart.

She pulled her daughter close and hugged her tight. Everything they were going through would be worth it. It had to be. "Sometimes I just need a good cry, Slugger. Do you know what I mean?"

Her daughter's forehead wrinkled with worry. "I've never seen you cry before. Not even when Daddy hurt your feelings."

"Everybody cries, honey. Even moms."

Zoe laid her head against Faith's chest and wrapped her arms around her mother's body. "Do we have to move again?"

Faith looked around the room. "I'm sorry, sweetie. We're packing up and getting out. Tonight."

THE DARK PANELING closed in on Burke. He hated this office, a mirror image of his father's. The mahogany desk, the leather chairs. All his life his father had wanted a carbon copy of himself. Burke had lived up to those expectations. He'd been happy to. In Burke's childhood eyes, his father had been the greatest man he'd ever known. He'd believed that until the age of sixteen.

Burke threw down the latest balance sheet. That was the year he'd fallen in love for the first time. With the *perfect* woman.

That was the year he'd uncovered his father's feet of clay.

That was the year Burke had been forced to kill the woman he loved.

He walked across the plush carpet and poured a drink.

The door opened without a knock. He whirled around, ready to tear into whoever dared interrupt his planning until he saw the woman who walked in with a smile on her face.

"Burke, darling, you shouldn't be working this late. I've told your father not to foist his bad habits onto you."

"Mother." Burke walked across the room and gently pulled her close. "I wasn't expecting you."

Her sweet smile tilted the corners of her mouth. "I'm dragging your father to the club for a late dinner. Do you want to join us?"

"I have work to do."

His mother pouted her lips. "You're too much like Gerard."

No, I'm not! he wanted to scream. "You always say that." He smiled.

She kissed his cheek and he released her. His mother deserved the world for putting up with his father all these years, for helping Burke survive his childhood. He'd do anything to protect her and to give her whatever would keep her life content and happy.

That had been true all his life. His vow had been put to the test when he'd discovered his father's weakness for other women, but Burke had passed the test.

She picked up the photo of Zoe on his desk. "I can't wait for your little girl to visit. Did she like the dress I sent her? I've been looking at a catalog. I think I'm too old-fashioned. I want Zoe to have a hip grandmother."

Inside, Burke winced. Until Orren brought Zoe back to him, he'd have to lie, and he hated lying to his mother. "You don't need to change a thing, Mom. Zoe loved the dress. She's planning to wear it next time she visits."

Of course, sometimes lies were necessary.

His mother frowned. "How long will Faith's trip last? I miss my granddaughter. I'm sure it's good for Zoe to attend a camp to help with her reading, but she's been gone all summer. School starts soon."

Burke hugged his mother to his side. "Zoe will be back before long. I promise."

She let out a slow sigh and replaced the photo. "I'm sorry your marriage to Faith didn't work out. She seemed like such a nice girl." She patted his cheek. "You look tired, Burke. You should find someone who can make you happy. Your father worries."

Hardly.

He kissed the perfectly coiffed hair. "I have work, and you have a date."

She flushed and patted his arm. "Don't work too hard, my sweet boy."

Burke escorted her to his office door and gave her one final kiss.

"I'll do what I have to do."

SEVEN IN THE morning didn't come early enough, especially when you'd bedded down the night before in a small grove of trees. Thank God Faith had made an emergency plan in case something like this happened. Zoe was safely hidden. Faith had stayed up all night clutching the bat, staring at the back of the shack where they'd lived for the past few months.

She stretched, and her body protested with every movement. Each time she blinked, she could have sworn sandpaper scraped off a layer of her eyelid.

Burke hadn't shown up, though she'd caught a glimpse of a couple of figures lurking around. Unfortunately, she hadn't been able to get a good look except that one appeared to be bald. Just like Zoe'd said.

If she'd harbored any last hope, it was gone. Burke had definitely found them.

Her daughter squirmed out of their hiding place and crawled over to Faith. "Is it time to get up?"

"Afraid so." She wrapped the blanket she'd been forced to steal from the shack's bedding around Zoe.

Her daughter rubbed her eyes and let out a yawn as big as Texas. "My stuff is still in the bag, isn't it?

We got everything? My unicorn? The baseball Daddy gave me?"

"It's all here."

"What if we left something?" Zoe asked.

"We didn't." Faith had no plans on ever going back to that shack. "Let's get ready."

Using water from a bottle, they cleaned up as best they could before the long walk into town. Faith took the backstreets and traveled across a vacant lot or two. No need to make their presence visible.

Zoe didn't skip along like normal, and Faith found it tough to smile or fake any optimism. They were in deep trouble. She tucked her money into her pocket except for one hundred dollars for gas. She just prayed the mechanic would cut her a break on the car repairs. Especially since he already had the ten grand she'd prepaid for the IDs.

Finally, Faith made out the siding of the auto shop. She gripped Zoe's hand and rounded the back of the building. A shiny new vehicle sat outside the small repair shop. At least Ray was early. She scanned the empty streets and tried the doorknob, but it was locked.

She pounded on the front door. It yanked open.

The guy looked like he'd done an all-nighter. Oil and grease streaked his jeans and work shirt.

"Oh, it's you," Ray said with a frown. "Come back next week. Car's not ready."

He moved to shut the door on her, but she stuck her foot through the crack.

"Not an option. I need to leave town." She shoved her way inside. "Zoe, stay out here, but where I can see you." She turned on Ray. "I need the car. And the other items. Today."

Faith crossed over to the counter and laid the envelope down.

Ray followed her. He fingered the bills and clicked his tongue. "You're $500 short."

"I know. But we have to go."

He shook his head. "No can do. Besides, I found another problem. It's gonna be another $750 before it's drivable. Parts, you know."

His twisted smile challenged her. Faith tried with everything in her not to react, not to cry out in defeat. She straightened her back. "This is all I have. You gave me a quote, and I've paid you a lot of money. You know I'll come through with the rest."

"Sorry," he said, though he didn't look sorry at all. "I can't give you the car without the full amount." He moved closer, his face just inches from her. "Besides, it don't matter. No IDs yet."

Her knees buckled. She gripped the counter to keep from sinking to the floor. "I need those IDs," Faith said, her voice rising.

His gaze scraped up and down her body. A horrible feeling slithered through Faith. She stepped away from him and crossed her arms over her chest. Lifting her chin, she met his gaze. "Then the deal's off. I want my money back. All of it."

She grabbed at the cash but he yanked it away.

"Hold on now." With a slimy smile painting his face, he leaned toward her. "I'll get the IDs in a couple of days. As to the car, well, maybe we can work something out." His smiled broadened. "A trade wouldn't be a bad idea."

"Mom?" Zoe called through the cracked open door.

Days? Faith stilled. Impossible. They couldn't return to the shack. Her mind whirled with possibilities. Mrs. Hargraves *might* help. Or maybe they could sneak in after closing and sleep in the library.

His smile broadened as if he knew he'd won. He leaned forward and lowered his voice. "Ditch the kid. Come back at noon. We'll have a little fun for the next few days until the documents arrive, and I'll give you the car when it's ready."

Faith swallowed deeply. She couldn't believe she was even entertaining the proposition.

Ray fingered a stray piece of her hair. "Just so we're clear, I've been very lonely lately. Your enthusiastic company would square the account. A fair trade."

He scooped up the cash from the counter and pocketed it. She now had $100 to her name. Ray had everything else.

"Mom?"

Could she let him touch her? For Zoe?

"I'll see you at noon, sweet cheeks." He leaned close and licked the edge of her jaw to her ear. "If you're not here, the sheriff will get an anonymous tip, and I don't think you want him to wonder about you. Sheriff Redmond's the curious type."

She couldn't hide her shudder. She hated that he assumed she'd comply. As much as she loathed to admit it, she wasn't sure he was wrong.

Faith would do anything for Zoe.

THE SUN HAD fully risen when Stefan paused outside the Carder Diner, his empty thermos at his side. He'd grown tired of burning his morning brew over a campfire. Besides, Carla had a way with coffee beans.

The post-dawn glow gave the huge expanse of sky a soft tint. The angry clouds of yesterday were a distant memory. He'd been forced to get used to the constant sun and blue sky here. He missed the rain of Bellevaux, but the truth was, he'd grown to like the drama of the West Texas landscape. He hadn't decided where he'd go after this, but he might want to stay where the sun wasn't constantly hidden by clouds.

He pushed through the restaurant door at eight in the morning. The sizzling of hot bacon and scent of fresh coffee evoked a groan of temptation. Out of habit, he scanned the seating, lingering on the rear exit and timing his escape from the building. He didn't anticipate trouble, but he doubted he'd ever break the habit. It had saved his life more than once.

When his gaze landed on the booth closest to the back door, he paused. Faith and Zoe sat at the table. Seemed he and the pair had one more thing in common.

Zoe dug into a plate of bacon and eggs while Faith watched her daughter, sipping on coffee, no plate in front of her. He walked over to his standard seat at the counter and took a sip from the cup Carla had placed at his usual stool before setting his thermos on the counter. Carla scooped it up to fill, but he didn't attempt a conversation with her. He had every intention of eavesdropping.

"Mom? Aren't you going to eat?" Zoe asked.

"Not today, honey." Faith's voice whispered with a quick look under her lashes at him. She flushed and dipped her gaze, stirring her coffee longer than anyone would need to.

So she'd seen him come in. No need for pretense. He grabbed his cup and slid into the booth adjacent to theirs. Her eyes widened. He lifted his cup and smiled at her.

"I don't like camping out in the bushes," Zoe complained. "I got prickles down my back. Will we get the car back today so we can sleep on the cushions?"

"Hush, Zoe. You know the car is broken. How about you use your inside voice and finish your breakfast. Please, Slugger."

The little girl shoveled more food in her mouth while Faith avoided his gaze. She clearly would have preferred he sit anywhere but within listening distance. Too bad. If she was homeless, he could at least do something about that.

He didn't bother to ask himself why he cared. Maybe she and Zoe reminded him of Jenny Jennings and her daughter. He'd been too late to save them. Was he simply trying to redeem himself?

Could be.

Faith lowered her head and stared into her coffee cup. Dark circles shadowed her eyes. Her mouth was tight with stress. Something was wrong, something more than yesterday.

"Will that man fix the car? That would be good. I'm tired of walking everywhere."

"Me, too." Faith cleared her throat. "You let me worry about the car."

"What did the man want to trade?"

Faith's gaze jerked up to her daughter's.

"You're going to go see him at noon. He said he was lonely and you could help him, but I don't get it. He wants to talk? He must be really sad. Maybe I should go with you. I'm a great talker. Everybody says so. I always get in trouble at school."

A lot of words in one breath. Stefan would be impressed with Zoe's soliloquy if Faith didn't appear quite so mortified.

"I know very well." Faith's skin tinged a strange green and her gaze darted around the room.

Stefan could have told her no one else but him heard Zoe's revelation. The moment he'd walked in, he'd mapped the location of every person in the diner. He studied his coffee so she wouldn't have to see the fury he doubted he could hide.

Zoe swallowed another bite. "We could play baseball with him. Baseball helps me when I feel lonely," she said between chews.

"I don't think baseball's what he has in mind."

No doubt there. Stefan had never liked Ray, and had never let him touch his SUV. Rumor was the man had a reputation of gouging customers who couldn't afford to take their car to San Angelo or San Antonio for repairs.

"You leave him to me, Slugger," Faith said. "And don't talk with your mouth full."

For Stefan, the bigger question was why hadn't Faith sought help from the law? He knew the answer. He and

Faith had a lot in common. He'd never go to the law if he had a choice. There were too many questions he couldn't answer. The idea of Faith feeling like she had no other options made Stefan want to knock most of Ray's teeth out. That she was considering giving in— and he could tell she was, just from the sick expression on her face—made him want to do even more damage. Preferably something that would cause Ray not to walk straight for a month or two.

Carla walked over to his table. "Changing things up on me, Léon?"

He pasted his standard charming smile on his face. "What can I say? I'm a man of mystery."

"I won't argue there. What'll you have?"

He ordered his usual, a couple of eggs, some bacon and a biscuit—he'd really miss her biscuits.

He motioned Carla closer and whispered his instructions in her ear. She grinned and hurried to the kitchen.

"I'm done," Zoe said, shoving her plate away. "I need to go to the bathroom."

Faith started to stand.

"M…o…o…om! I can go by myself."

Stefan bit back a smile. Faith's daughter made him smile. The girl had backbone.

For the next few minutes, Faith avoided looking his way by watching the door of the restroom.

Stefan emptied his coffee cup. He wasn't quite sure how to approach Faith. If their positions were reversed he certainly wouldn't want some stranger to stick her nose where it didn't belong.

Before he could solve the dilemma, Carla set the

filled thermos in front of him, followed by his break-fast. The aroma of bacon caused his belly to rumble.

He tucked into his eggs, keeping an eye out for Carla. The waitress better hurry before Faith and Zoe left.

The little girl rushed back from the bathroom. Instead of sliding into the next booth, she stopped right beside Stefan. "Hi. I saw you in the library yesterday."

"That you did." Stefan smiled at the little girl. "You were a big help."

"Zoe," Faith hissed.

The little pistol shrugged at him and slunk back to their booth.

"How was your breakfast, sweetie?" Carla asked Zoe.

"Yummy."

The waitress placed a full plate in front of Faith.

"What's this?" she asked.

"Breakfast," Carla said.

"I… I can't afford it," Faith whispered.

"It's already been paid for, honey. Accept the gift." Carla winked at Stefan and walked away.

Faith stared over Zoe's head at him. "You did this?" she asked.

"Sounds like you're having a rough morning." Stefan hesitated, but truth was, he didn't have the time or patience to be polite, and if she had a noon dead-line, neither did Faith. "Ray's got a reputation. I can talk to—"

"Zoe," Faith interrupted. "Wash your hands."

"I already did—"

Faith quirked her brow. "Really?"

Zoe bowed and shook her head. "No."

"That's what I thought. Now go."

Once Zoe was out of earshot, Faith pinched her nose. "Look, I appreciate the gesture, but…"

"I get it. You don't know me from Adam…or Ray, but I can help you. If you'll let me."

Chapter Three

Dishes crashed behind the counter. The entire diner went silent except for the pop of splattered oil from the grill in the kitchen.

The sound of shattering plates had nothing to do with Faith going speechless, though. Léon deserved that honor. She forced herself to close her mouth, fallen open from utter shock.

"Sorry, folks," Carla said with a sheepish grin. "Go back to your breakfast."

The volume of low conversation and clattering silverware rose at a steady pace in the busy eatery.

Faith couldn't stop staring at the man facing her.

Léon—like she'd ever forget that name—didn't avert his gaze; he just sat looking at her, unflinching, his expression deadly serious. Faith couldn't believe a man she'd barely met—who had obviously been eavesdropping—would show any interest in them, much less offer to help. Things like that didn't happen. Especially not to her.

The one time she'd bought into a too-good-to-be-true offer, she'd found herself married to Burke.

Léon left his half-eaten plate and scooted into Zoe's seat. "Who are you running from?"

"This is crazy. You're crazy." She placed her hands flat on the table. "You don't even know me."

Léon leaned against the seat, too relaxed from her perspective. "I have a job that puts me in contact with people who are in trouble, and Faith, you're wearing trouble all over your face. I'd like to help because I think you need it."

He reached across the table and took her hands in his. "Talk to me."

Stunned by his action, she didn't immediately pull away from him. His hands held hers with gentle warmth, not the harsh force Burke had used. For a moment, she allowed herself to feel that unfamiliar human touch even as she knew she couldn't ask for anything. Despite Mrs. Hargraves's endorsement yesterday, Faith couldn't risk trusting anyone else. Burke was too dangerous. More dangerous than she'd ever thought a human being could be.

She tugged her hands away and he let her go. "You're just guessing. You can't know."

He didn't say a word, just quirked a brow.

"I appreciate the offer, but I can't. I won't. You won't want any part of my troubles."

A glint of humor lit his eyes. "I can handle myself. I've faced more bad guys than pickups in Carder."

She couldn't stop the small smile. "You've been busy, then, since every other car I've seen in this town is a pickup."

"You get my point then." He leaned toward her. "I

have significant resources at my disposal. You don't have to go into this battle alone."

At one time Faith would have given anything to find someone to share her problems with, someone to rely on, but she didn't believe in fairy tales anymore, and she'd accepted the truth. She was on her own. She and her daughter.

Zoe opened the bathroom door. Faith stood up. "I appreciate the offer, Léon, but it's not fair to drag you into our problems. Zoe and I are leaving Carder today. It was nice to meet you. And thank you for breakfast."

She grabbed two backpacks and held out her hand to Zoe, trying not to let her panic show. She recognized the questioning furrow of her daughter's forehead, but after a well-understood look, Zoe bit her lip and took Faith's hand.

They'd been out in public far too long. Hopefully if anyone came asking for her, Carder would live up to its reputation and be silent. Faith had until noon to figure out what to do about her car. Either way, as far as Léon and Carder, Texas, were concerned, Faith and Zoe would be gone. "We're leaving."

She made her way to the back door and walked into the heat of the late summer morning.

Zoe gave Léon an apologetic smile. "Bye."

He followed them out the back of the diner. "Whoever's after you knows you're here, doesn't he? That's why you're leaving today."

She ignored him and shifted one backpack on her shoulder before handing the smaller one to Zoe. "Goodbye, Léon."

Faith led her daughter down an alley leading to the library. She forced herself not to look behind her until she'd walked a full block. Work started at nine, and she had until noon to make an untenable decision.

With a quick pause, she allowed herself to glance back.

"He's gone," Zoe said from beside her. "I liked him. He was nice."

"Maybe." Faith knelt in front of Zoe. "But for now it's you and me, Slugger. Okay?"

"Okay, Mom. You and me."

WELL, THAT HAD gone well. The morning air carried the scent of rain, but for the second straight day Stefan didn't take the time to notice. He rounded the diner and stalked to his SUV. Faith had schooled him a new lesson on women in trouble: offering to help was the quickest way to scare them away. Particularly if she was on the run.

What got him was she really believed she was somehow protecting him. He rubbed his brow to alleviate the headache starting to build behind his eyes. She'd made herself perfectly clear. She didn't want his help. He should listen to her.

Besides, in three days, Léon would be dead.

In three days, his life in Carder would be over and his new life would begin.

In three days, he'd leave Faith and Zoe behind.

His vehicle's engine revved, and he pulled into the street. He should stay on the road out of town and drive straight to CTC's headquarters, let Ransom know his plans and prepare for a new future.

He didn't have anyone to tell. Only two members of CTC along with his sister and her husband even knew he was alive.

Maybe he could leave a gift for his nieces and nephew since CTC was located on the Triple C, his brother-in-law's ranch. Eventually his sister and her family would make their way to the spread. Maybe he could even risk calling his sister Kat before he vanished again.

That's exactly what he should do. Instead, when he drove past the library, he slowed down. Faith and Zoe hurried toward the front door. Faith glanced over her shoulder every few seconds. Her gaze paused at his vehicle. She turned her back on him, knelt down and whispered at Zoe before knocking on the library door. Mrs. Hargraves opened up with a smile.

Faith ducked inside and Zoe gave him a cheery wave before placing her finger over her lips and disappearing after her mother. That smile and mischievous attitude reminded him of his niece.

Of course, the last time he'd seen Lanie in person had been years ago. She didn't know him except from photographs. He didn't know if his sister had told her kids he was dead, or just never mentioned him.

Lanie was fearless from what he remembered. Zoe put on a good front, but he could see Faith's fear clouded her daughter's outlook.

With a curse, he jerked the vehicle into gear and made a U-turn toward the auto repair shop.

The siding had seen better days, but Stefan caught sight of a brand-new Land Rover out back, so money was flowing from somewhere.

Stefan peered through the glass on the front door. Ray counted bills at his counter, a satisfied smile on his face. Eager to wipe away the grin, Stefan slammed open the door.

The bell thwacked against the glass. Ray shoved the money into his cash drawer. He looked up. "Can I help you?"

"I hear you've got a car back there you've been holding hostage for a trade? Did I get that right, Ray?"

The man flushed. "What's it to you?"

Stefan leaned across the desk. "Oh, it means a lot to me, actually. What does she owe?"

"A thousand bucks."

"Show me the invoice," Stefan ordered.

Ray dug through a large pile of papers and thrust a document at Stefan. "It's not complete. We found a leak—"

"Save it. I know exactly what you're doing." Stefan scanned the list of repairs. "She's paid you enough. Give me the keys." He held out his hand.

"But it's not fixed. I don't got the parts."

"You want to play this hard, I'm happy to oblige." Stefan turned and flipped the Open sign to Closed. He locked the front door and pulled down all the shades.

Ray's face paled. Stefan crossed his arms in front of him. "Let me explain the situation so even you can understand it, Ray. Faith is a friend of mine. I don't like

it when my friend is gouged by a small-time criminal."
He rounded the counter. "Do you know who I am?"

The guy shook his head.

Stefan smiled. "Let's just say that I know how to
make a man beg for his life and still not do any visible
damage. Would you like me to demonstrate?"

Ray's eyes widened with terror.

"I didn't think so. Now get out there and finish those
repairs. In fact, I'll watch you."

Stefan followed a shaking Ray out to the car. Within
thirty minutes the mechanic had the car purring as well
as a thirty-year-old car could. He shoved the keys into
Stefan's hand. "So, why are you going to all this trouble for her? She putting out for you?"

Stefan didn't hesitate. He grabbed the idiot's collar
and shoved him against the wall. "You disrespect her
like that again, and I'll teach you some manners. Oh,
and Ray. You might want to straighten up your act.
I'm paying a visit to Sheriff Redmond the moment I
leave this place."

Ray lifted his chin in misplaced defiance. "I
wouldn't do that if I were you. Not unless you want
your lady friend to get into trouble."

Stefan stilled before tightening his grip. "And why
would that be?"

"W-we have a side deal. She hasn't received deliv-
ery."

"What deal?" Stefan's words came out clipped. He
should have known there was more to this than a car.
"I'm waiting."

Stefan didn't remove his hand, but pressed his forearm against the man's windpipe.

"N-none of your—" Ray clutched at Stefan's arms and sucked in a breath. "Business."

"I'm putting about eleven pounds of pressure against your trachea. At thirty-three pounds, I'll crush it, and don't think I can't. I'm not even breaking a sweat."

"Wh-who are you?"

"I'm a ghost," Stefan said with a small grin. "I don't exist."

Ray clawed at Stefan's arm. He didn't budge.

"You're turning blue, Ray. I suggest you talk. I wouldn't risk testing my patience."

"I'll…call…the…sheriff," he gasped.

"Go right ahead. We'll see what Sheriff Redmond thinks about you gouging your customers and running an illegal business out of your shop."

"You don't have proof."

"You told me your customers don't mention your deals with them. You admitted you have the leverage to gouge them and they don't have anywhere to go. Simple math, Ray."

The mechanic sagged, clutching at Stefan's hands to keep upright. "I can't breathe. Let me go. I'll tell you everything."

"That's better." Stefan eased the pressure some, but not completely. "I'm listening."

"You don't understand. I do business with people who… Well, they expect a certain amount of volume. This is a small town. Sometimes, I run short, so I—"

"Blackmail people who can't afford to say no. I understand. I want names."

Ray shook his head. "I can't. They'll kill me."

"And I won't?" Stefan asked.

"No offense, but they scare me more than you do. I get the feeling you play by a set of rules at least. These guys? They got no rules."

Stefan released Ray. The man bent over, sucking air as if his life depended on it. Stefan had to end-run his fear. "What did Faith buy from you?"

Easy question to answer, and the floodgates opened. Ray told him everything. In fact, he wouldn't stop talking.

After listening to the idiot for a solid fifteen minutes, Stefan kneaded the back of his neck. "Shut up, Ray."

Stefan picked up the phone and dialed a familiar number.

"Léon." Ransom Grainger, his boss and head of CTC, answered. "What's up? You got something to share?"

CTC's boss man was damn spooky. "You figured out I'm leaving." Stefan couldn't keep the resignation from his voice.

"I had a feeling. Annie helping you?"

"It's the only way," Stefan said. "I've been living on borrowed time, and we both know it."

The crick of a chairback filtered through the phone.

"You sure you want to start over completely? Last time, you were able to keep a little of your past alive.

Similar job, we kept you in the know about your sister and her family..."

"If I stay my life will always be in the shadows. Eventually I'll bring my trouble to Carder. We both know that."

"Maybe. But if it comes we can handle it."

"I won't take the risk, Ransom. You and CTC have too much to lose. Now, do you want my tip or not?"

Ransom bit out a curse. "This conversation isn't over, Stefan."

"Yes, it is." Stefan cleared his throat. "Got a lead on some smugglers who deal in guns and stolen identities and have a contact in Carder. You interested?"

"Definitely. And Léon, we'll talk soon, I assume?"

"Of course." He'd miss working with Ransom. With everyone.

"Good. Now back to business. Firepower?"

"Unknown, but a lot," Stefan reported. "They've got a pipeline through the auto shop in town."

"Ray." Ransom let out a harsh curse. "I should've known. Consider it taken care of."

Stefan ended the call and pinned Ray with his gaze. "You'll be receiving a visit from a couple of my friends. You tell them everything. You do exactly what they say, and you may get out of this alive. Do you understand?"

Ray nodded his head.

"If you cooperate, you may, and I stress *may*, be able to escape this mess without jail time. Do you understand?"

He nodded again.

"If you so much as step a toe out of line from now

on, I'll be back, and this time you'll wish you were facing your business partners. Do you understand?"

Ray shook his head up and down. "Yes, sir."

"Good." Stefan punched him in the gut and kneed him so he'd sing soprano for a week.

Ray dropped to the floor and held his groin. He looked up at Stefan.

"That's for insulting Faith." Stefan stared at the man. "And by the way. She'd never let a toad like you touch her."

THE MORNING WAS half over already, too quickly as far as Faith was concerned. She sat at the side of the library, strategically perched behind a tree, ever watchful of her surroundings. She hadn't noticed any unfamiliar vehicles and no strangers had come into the library so far, but she could barely breathe for the tension knotting her back.

What was she going to do? They couldn't stay in Carder, and she had one hour to make her decision.

Even if she agreed to do what Ray wanted, could she trust him to keep up his end of the bargain?

Stupid question, with an obvious answer. Of course not.

Faith's entire body shook with strain. She couldn't let Burke get to Zoe. She needed a solution and making Ray angry meant not getting their new identity. She'd paid $10,000 for a new life—the only way she could protect Zoe.

She was trapped.

Léon's offer reverberated in her mind, but she'd be taking a huge risk. Could she trust him?

Why was she even considering his offer?

Her head hurt as the flurry of questions pounded against her skull. She gripped her hair. She knew why: because one hour and one hundred dollars wouldn't get her out of town and away from Burke.

Zoe raced past her. "I found the bunny, Mom. I'll catch it this time." She held up a small box and dove behind a hedge. Faith wasn't too worried about the bunny since Zoe and the rabbit played the identical game every day.

The city hall clock chimed eleven like an alarm sounding a warning. Faith rubbed her face with her hands. The key to the front door of the library burned in her pocket. She'd taken it from Mrs. Hargraves's desk. The betrayal ate at her, but she couldn't ask Zoe to sleep outside again. They'd been lucky last night, but more thunderstorms were coming in from the east.

They could leave and sneak in after her boss closed up then be gone around daylight. The food she'd packed might last a few days.

Only one problem left. Giving in to Ray, or tucking her tail between her legs and asking Léon to help.

Zoe hopped from behind a tree and ran across the sidewalk at full speed, skidding on her sneakers to a halt. She knelt down on the sidewalk in front of Faith, drew a hopscotch board with chalk, then grabbed one of her polished rocks from her knapsack.

"Wanna play, Mom?" she asked.

"In a minute, Slugger."

Zoe sidled up to her mother. "What's wrong?"

Faith clung to her daughter, the warmth of her small body filling her with comfort and hope. "It'll be fine. You play one round, and I'll join you."

Zoe bounced over to the game and slid the rock along the concrete.

The library's front door opened. Mrs. Hargraves stepped out and peered around before catching sight of Faith tucked behind the tree. She made her way down the library steps and over to them. "You're looking worried."

Faith chewed on her lip. "We have to leave."

"He found you?" the librarian asked, her eyes dark with concern.

Faith nodded.

"Then why aren't you already gone?" Her boss's eyes widened with realization. "Your car?"

"It's complicated." She watched Zoe jump through her hopscotch board. Faith sent the older woman a sidelong glance. "Léon offered to help me. I turned him down."

"Why would you do a fool thing like that, girl?"

The incredulity in Mrs. Hargraves's voice would've made Faith smile if she'd had it in her. "I don't know him. No one offers a handout without wanting something in return. And you know what I mean."

Her boss plopped down on the planter next to Faith and crossed one boot over the other. "Ninety percent of the time, you're probably right. If you're talking about Ray the auto-moron, you're definitely right. That boy was a problem from the time he was three. I kicked him out of the library permanently when he turned thirteen. Selling joints between the stacks." Mrs. Hargraves huffed in disgust, snagged a stone from the ground and flicked it into the adjacent rock garden. "Léon is different. He wouldn't have told you this, but he works with those boys out on the old Triple C Ranch. They've accomplished more than one miracle. If I was in bad trouble and needed someone…special, I'd call them up."

"I don't like relying on other people," Faith admitted. "I've been burned every time."

"At least you divorced him, honey. I had to wait for mine to die on me." Mrs. Hargraves winked.

Faith couldn't help but chuckle. "That's a story you haven't told me."

"Oh, it's not worth telling. He was an SOB and I married him because I was a ninny of nineteen." The librarian stood up, her spine stiff. "Call Léon."

She rounded the front of the library before freezing, her gaze pinned toward Main Street. "Faith, you said you turned Léon down?"

She nodded.

"I don't think he listened."

Faith peeked out from behind the tree. Mrs. Hargraves pointed down the street.

Her hunk-of-junk car headed their way with Léon at the wheel. He pulled in front of the library and stepped out of the vehicle. Ray followed in a large SUV. He parked behind Faith's car and without a word, hightailed in the direction of his garage at full speed, noticeably panicked.

Zoe ran over to Léon. "Our car! Look, Mom. He brought it back."

Faith's mouth opened wide. She didn't know what to say.

He ruffled Zoe's hair and strode up to Faith. "We need to talk." He handed her the keys and glanced down at Zoe. "In private."

Mind spinning, Faith gave a quick nod.

"I'll watch her, dear," the older woman said. "In fact, I may join her. You go inside to my office. And be nice. He's a good boy."

He arched his brow at Mrs. Hargraves, but she simply laughed. "You be nice, too, Léon. She's had a rough morning."

Side by side, they walked into the library and headed to her boss's office.

"I don't understand," she said once she'd closed them inside the small room. "How did you get my car? It was undrivable."

"Ray fixed it in thirty minutes. He's no longer an issue."

Faith sank into the chair in front of Mrs. Hargraves's desk. They *could* leave, if only for one thing.

"Did Ray give you anything else?" she asked in a hesitant voice.

"You mean your $10,000 deal?" Léon hitched his hip on the desk. "That's a bit of a problem. His business partner wanted double or you wouldn't get the IDs, and I've got to be honest, I doubt they'd pass for authentic."

Faith twisted her hands in her lap, denial running through her. "This can't be happening." She wrapped her arms around her body and rocked back and forth, her mind awhirl.

"Am I safe in assuming you don't have the money?"

With a sarcastic laugh she pulled a few crumpled bills from her back pocket. "This is it. One hundred bucks. That's all I have. Ray might as well want a million."

Léon plucked Mrs. Hargraves's chair from behind her desk and sat across from Faith. "Why do you and Zoe need new identities?

The keys dug into Faith's palm. She shook her head.

He took her hands in his and squeezed her chilled fingers. "Who are you running from, Faith?"

"You don't understand. His family is too powerful. We have no choice but to disappear."

"I may have a solution—"

She shook her head side to side. She couldn't listen. "We *can't* stay. He knows where we are. He trashed our place last night. I'll have to find another place to hide until I can raise the money. Maybe if I were closer to Mexico, I could find someone—"

"Take this." Léon released her hands and pulled out a thick folded envelope from his pocket. "You're making a mistake, but here's your $10,000." He pressed it into her hand.

She opened the envelope and peeked inside. "I don't understand."

He shrugged. "Ray realized he wasn't doing the right thing."

She slapped her hand to her mouth. Her eyes glistened. "I don't think you could possibly know what this means. You've saved our lives."

Impulsively, she leaned over and hugged him. "Thank you. Again."

For a moment he stiffened against her, before folding his arms around her. She'd meant the embrace to be a quick thank-you. Faith didn't expect the warmth that seeped through her body as he held her.

He bent his head to her ear. "Let me help you."

The breath behind his soft words tickled her ear. Her heart thudded against her chest in an anticipation she hadn't experienced in a very long time.

"You've done enough." She eased away from him. "You've given us hope."

"Stop! Leave her alone!" Mrs. Hargraves shouted.

Faith's eyes widened. She sprinted to the library door, and Léon raced past her in a full-on run. He slammed the heavy oak open. Faith stared in horror at the street.

An old Cadillac idled half on, half off the sidewalk. Mrs. Hargraves lay sprawled on the concrete, struggling to get up. A bald man held Zoe in his arms next to the vehicle. Her daughter fought like hell against him, kicking and screaming.

"Stop!" she shouted. "Zoe!"

Léon sprinted down the steps, but before he could reach Zoe, the man shoved her into the back seat of the car and dove into the vehicle. Zoe fought to open the door, but he must've locked it. She pounded her fists against the glass, but no sound penetrated.

With a shout, Léon vaulted onto the hood and

reached around to the driver's side. The guy twisted the steering wheel hard. Léon grabbed on. The car swerved again. He flew off and skidded across the asphalt.

Faith raced at the vehicle, but it was no use. The Cadillac sped away.

Her knees shook. Panting, she bent over and stared down the road. This couldn't be happening.

Zoe's panicked face peered through the back window.

And just like that, her daughter was gone.

Chapter Four

Tar and rock pressed into Stefan's palms. A wild screech sounded and the Cadillac disappeared around the first corner. He heaved to his feet, and without hesitation, sprinted to his SUV.

"Are you okay?" Faith rushed over, meeting him at the vehicle.

He'd love to slam his fist into the jaw of that baldheaded kidnapper. He couldn't believe he'd been too late. Again.

This time, though—unlike the Jennings family— he had a chance to save Zoe. He yanked open the car's door and cranked the key. Faith jumped into the passenger seat and buckled her seat belt.

He didn't try to argue. If Zoe were his, he'd have done the same thing.

"They'll be heading out of town." Stefan gunned the accelerator and swerved around the corner. "Where's he taking her?"

"Dallas," Faith said, her voice thick with unshed emotion. "That man was following us yesterday. His name is Jerry. I think he works for my ex-husband."

"Zoe's father?" A flood of curses coursed through Stefan's head.

"It's not what you think," she rushed out.

A man who'd pay a thug to terrify his child didn't win any Father of the Year awards. Stefan would figure it out later. First things first. He had to get Zoe back.

He headed east, but the car wasn't visible. He had a fifty-fifty chance and needed to up the odds. Stefan grabbed his phone and dialed.

In one ring he received an answer through his earpiece.

"Sheriff Blake Redmond."

"It's Léon." He quickly gave Blake a sitrep. "Best guess is the kidnapper's headed to Dallas. Can your deputies cut off his exit routes?"

"Cops?" she whispered, clutching his arm.

"We don't have a choice," Stefan mouthed. He hit the outskirts of Carder and floored the accelerator. The SUV zipped down the narrow road, the flat brush whizzing past. "I'm headed that way now."

"I don't have enough cars to cover all the roads," Blake said. "I bet he'll take Highway 113 to 67, unless he knows the area."

The squawk of a radio shrieked through the phone. "Deputy Smithson's patrolling west of town. I'll head your way." Blake shouted instructions to inform the other deputies of the situation. Drawers and cabinets slammed. "What's he driving?"

Stefan provided the make and model of the car and a description of the perp. "Plates were splattered with mud," he said. "Contact CTC for a chopper and some men. They'll give us more eyes surrounding Carder. And can you patch me through to Smithson? I've got an idea if he's not too far from Old Mine Road."

"I like the way you think," Blake said.

A few clicks signaled the call forward. Stefan glanced at Faith through the corner of his eye. She'd leaned forward in her seat and gripped the dashboard, straining as if ready to catapult through the window.

"Where is she?" Faith bit her lip, her eyes lined with worry.

"Not far." If the guy hadn't doubled back. Stefan couldn't push the car any faster. "Is Jerry from Dallas?"

"He was a bouncer at a bar in Weatherford."

"Which means he won't know the shortcuts." They had a chance.

"Léon, what do you need?" The deputy's voice came through Stefan's earpiece.

"A roadblock across 113. I want to force the guy onto Old Mine Road."

"The arroyo will box him in." Sirens sounded through the phone. "How far ahead is he?"

"I'm doing ninety. He had about four minutes on us."

"I'll set up at the fork on 113. You know it?"

"Perfect." Stefan yanked the steering wheel onto a dirt road. Six-foot-tall rows of sorghum nearly ready for harvest lined the route.

Faith bounced in the seat. "What are you doing? He wouldn't have gone this way."

"Trust me. It's a shortcut."

"What if you're wrong?" Faith gripped the armrest. "What if he didn't come this way?"

"There aren't that many ways leading out of Carder." Stefan winced at his reassurance. He'd made mistakes before, but this could be their only shot.

Within a few minutes a sheriff's office SUV, lights flashing, appeared on the horizon behind them.

"It's taking too long." Faith searched the horizon around them. Dirt flew from the rear wheels.

"If Jerry's taken the fastest way to Dallas, he'll go through San Angelo. Deputy Smithson's car will block the road just a few miles as the crow flies. We'll get him."

Stefan's phone rang.

"Cadillac in sight," the deputy said. "He's slowing down."

"Almost there," Stefan whispered.

"He turned, Léon."

Stefan made a quick right. Deep arroyos lined one side of Old Mine Road. He had to be smart about this. Zoe was in that car. He planted his truck in the center of the narrow road. Like clockwork, over a small rise, the Cadillac sped toward him.

Faith gasped. "You were right."

The car heading straight at them didn't swerve. Stefan braced himself, his foot hovered over the gas pedal.

The kidnapper veered at the last minute away from the deep ditch. His vehicle skidded across the dirt and into the brush before shuddering to a halt.

Stefan didn't hesitate. He grabbed a rifle from the back seat and rushed to the driver's side. He aimed at the guy's head. "Hands on the steering wheel," he shouted. "Use your elbow to roll down the window and unlock the doors. Don't try anything." He tapped the windshield with the barrel. "I won't miss."

Jerry's hands quaked as he complied. Still holding his weapon on the man, Stefan opened the back door. "Go to your mom, Zoe."

The little girl sprinted, arms pumping as hard as they could, to Faith. She hugged her daughter and ran her hands up and down the girl. "Are you okay?"

Zoe wrapped her arms around her mother and nodded.

Certain they were safe, Stefan studied his prisoner. Hired hand at best. He yanked the door and it bounced open. "Who ordered you to take the girl? Was it her father?"

"I can't." The man shook his head. "He'll kill me."

Flashing lights screamed toward them. Stefan cursed. He wanted the guy's name, and he didn't have confidence Faith would tell him. Come to think of it, he didn't even know Faith and Zoe's last name.

The realization conjured a twinge of admiration. She'd been more than careful. Faith had shown herself to be smart and savvy. More so than he'd given her credit for.

Deputy Smithson limped over and cuffed Jerry. The guy glared at Faith. "It won't matter," he shouted at her. "We're both dead anyway."

"Not yet, I'm not," Faith countered, positioning herself in front of Zoe. "And I don't plan on giving you or him the satisfaction."

Stefan strode over to her. "Take Zoe to the truck," he said with a tilt of his head. "I'll deal with this guy."

Faith led her daughter away, and Stefan followed her with his gaze. He liked Faith. He liked how protective she was of Zoe. He liked her fighting spirit. He'd also learned a very important detail about the gravity of her situation: Faith's ex-husband evoked real fear in a man who wasn't exactly a lightweight. Stefan needed to get the truth out of Jerry—hopefully enough to arrest Faith's ex.

Before he could begin questioning his prisoner, Blake Redmond's SUV rounded the curve and pulled to a stop near Stefan. He exited the vehicle. "Everyone okay?"

"Zoe is fine. So is her mom. Unfortunately, our friend Jerry, no last name—" Stefan indicated the kidnapper "—doesn't have a scratch on him."

Blake grabbed his phone and ordered the searchers and the CTC chopper to stand down. He pulled out his notebook. "I received a call from dispatch. Mrs. Hargraves is at the clinic. She's doing well. Of course, she's arguing with the doctor. She wants to go back to the library, but they're keeping her for observation for a bump on the head."

"Sounds just like her. Faith will be relieved."

The sheriff tipped his Stetson back from his brow. "She know who did this?" He stared at Stefan's vehicle where Faith and Zoe huddled in the back seat.

Stefan didn't blink. Blake was a straight-arrow kind of law officer, but he also understood about family, and justice.

"Her ex."

"I hate custody disputes." Blake's forehead furrowed in concentration. "What's your take?"

"She's got reason to be scared." Stefan stroked his jaw. "Can you hold this guy without their statement? At least until I get the full picture?"

Blake hooked his thumb in his belt loop near his badge. "I *should* take her in now. You know that."

From the tone in Blake's voice, Stefan could tell he understood. CTC had worked with the sheriff before. He valued the law's intent—and justice—more than the letter.

"Give me a day or two, Blake. This is more than a straightforward custody battle. If I'm wrong, I'll bring her to you myself."

Blake slapped his hat against his thigh. "Our prisoner abducted a child in front of witnesses in broad daylight. He won't be leaving my jail anytime soon." The sheriff paused before meeting Stefan's gaze. "You've got two days. After that, I won't be able to stop the legal wheels."

Stefan glanced over his shoulder at Faith's skittish expression. "I hope it's enough."

MIDMORNING LIGHT BOUNCED off Burke's immaculately polished mahogany desk. His feet sank into the thick carpet. He'd been here all night, waiting for word. He hadn't stopped pacing. Any minute now he should get the phone call that his daughter would be coming home.

Once he got hold of her, he could control her.

Of course, Faith would never see Zoe again. Burke would make certain of it.

His cell phone rang.

"Thomas."

"Jerry got caught. He's in jail in Carder, Texas, on kidnapping charges."

Burke let out a stream of curses. "How could you let this happen?"

"Don't blame me. You're the one who recommended the guy. *You* said I could trust him. Well, he's not as advertised. The idiot ransacked her house. To intimidate her, he told me. Instead, she ran. Made things twice as difficult to grab your daughter."

"Where's Zoe? Did you get her?"

"Jerry had her for all of fifteen minutes before the local sheriff returned her to her mother. We're on the sheriff's radar, and I haven't identified any Thomas, Inc. strings you can pull."

"What's this Podunk sheriff's name?" Burke picked up a letter opener and slid the edge across his palm. In his mind, he imagined blood oozing from the wound. The image transformed into his ex-wife's throat, exsanguinating her until her lifeless body fell to the floor. "My father doesn't need to know about this. You understand?"

"Double my fee, you'll buy my silence, and I'll take care of Sheriff Redmond. And my loyalty."

Burke's neck muscles bunched in protest, but for now he needed Orren's expertise.

"Have you located Faith and Zoe?"

"They left the scene with some cowboy playing hero. No intel on him. He's a wild card."

Burke fell into his leather chair and drummed his

fingers across his desk. The guy was a loose end he couldn't afford. In fact, there were too many loose ends all the way around. They'd *all* have to be taken care of eventually. "Clean up this mess. Jerry knows me."

"You pay me to make problems disappear. But from now on, I do the hiring. I do the terminating."

Burke spun in his chair and peered across the Dallas downtown skyline. "Fine."

"I'll take care of Jerry and bring your daughter to you." Orren paused. "If your ex gets in the way?"

"I want *my* wife gone. Disappeared. With no trace."

"You certain about that? Your father—"

"Faith is *my* business. Not his," Burke said, his shoulders tight with anger. He pitched back two fingers of whiskey. "Just make certain I'm not implicated."

"Triple my fee and I'll take care of her myself. Within twenty-four hours your daughter will be with you and your ex-wife will be dead."

The West Texas landscape surrounding Stefan's vehicle stretched out for an eternity. The midday sun beat down on them. When he'd first arrived in West Texas, he hadn't realized the horizon rested sixty and in some places even one hundred miles away. Most didn't.

Stefan glanced in the rearview mirror. Faith held Zoe snuggled in her arms. The little girl had fallen asleep clutching her mother. Faith stroked her daughter's hair, tension lining her mouth. He didn't blame her for being scared. He might not be a father, but he couldn't imagine anything worse than having a child taken from you, even if it had only been for a half hour.

Zoe stretched and blinked open her eyes. "Where are we going?"

"Camping," Stefan responded, meeting Faith's gaze in the mirror. "Do you like camping?"

"Will we sleep in your truck?" Zoe asked. "Mom and I went camping in the car after we left home."

Faith winced at her daughter's words.

"We'll stay in a tent."

"Cool. I spent the night in a tent in my best friend Danny's backyard." She yawned again.

"Try to sleep, Zoe. We didn't get much rest last night," Faith whispered.

The little girl sagged against her mother and soon her breathing evened out. Faith, on the other hand, fought back a yawn and kept her gaze focused out the back window.

Stefan turned onto another dirt road, searching the landscape for any signs of dust that wasn't caused by his SUV.

"So far so good," he said in a low voice so as not to wake Zoe. "We're not being followed."

He'd taken all the precautions he could. He'd stowed everything they owned in the back of his truck only after he'd swept the items for tracking devices. Since her ex possessed enough resources to hire a man to locate them in Carder and to kidnap Zoe, he could only think of two places where they would be safe. His camp or the CTC compound. The moment he'd mentioned CTC and the ex-military covert operatives who frequented the place, Faith had shut down, so he'd piled them into his SUV.

She met Stefan's gaze in the mirror, apprehensive at best. "Does the sheriff know where we'll be?"

Her concern for law enforcement hadn't been lost on Stefan. He needed to understand why. They'd be having a long conversation soon. "No one knows. I like my privacy."

"Good." Finally, Faith relaxed against the seat. Within minutes, her eyes had closed, her lashes fanning the shadows beneath her eyes. For the first time since Stefan had met her, the tightness around her mouth eased a bit, and her face took on a softness he found far too appealing.

Stefan drove for another half hour and took several more intentional wrong turns before doubling back. If anyone had wanted to track him, they wouldn't be able to.

Just after noon he felt comfortable enough to exit a dirt road. He headed toward the small rock outcropping that protected his campsite from the weather. A small stream trickled through a creek bed to the north. It hadn't been easy to find a water source out here, but Stefan had managed.

He pulled up near the midsized tent and opened the door. A blast of hot air hit him full throttle. "We're here," he said, exiting the SUV.

Faith yawned and helped Zoe out of the truck.

The little girl's eyes widened in surprise and she spun around. A huge grin split her face. "This is awesome. Can we fish?"

"The creek's not deep enough," Stefan said.

Her smile fell.

"We might find some frogs," he offered. "And I've seen a horned toad or two wandering around."

"Neat."

The midday Texas sun burned bright in the sky, beating down. His campfire lay dormant, his cooler in the tent to keep it from being pelted by the summer day. Stefan pulled out a couple of camp chairs from the back of his SUV and placed them in a small shaded area. He retrieved cold water from the cooler and handed one each to Faith and Zoe.

After sitting down, Faith took a swig. "How did you ever find this place?"

"I spent a lot of hours searching the backcountry. One night after a long day's ride, an afternoon storm blew in. The sun was setting and I headed toward these rocks. I stay here when I come to town."

"You don't have a house?" Zoe bent down and picked up a piece of quartz and shoved it into her pocket.

He doubted she'd consider the palace where he grew up quite the same thing. He sat across from them. "I travel a lot for my job. It's easier to camp out than worry about keeping up a place. Besides, there's never a no vacancy sign out here."

The corners of Faith's lips lifted, and her eyes crinkled. She lit up when she smiled. He shouldn't notice, but he couldn't help himself. Something about her...

"I like it here. Maybe we should camp out, too, Mom." Zoe sipped her water and handed the bottle to her mother. "Can I explore?"

"Make sure you can always see the tent." Faith took the beverage and set it on the ground.

Zoe huffed an exasperated sigh. "I'm not a baby." She raced around the camp, bending to pick some flowers, then checking out a cactus.

"She doesn't stop, does she?" Stefan said, watching the little girl dart when anything new caught her attention. "How do you keep up?"

"I don't."

He glanced over at Zoe practicing opening and closing the tent's zipper. At least she played far enough away for him to ask a few questions.

If only he could find the right words not to send an extremely skittish Faith back behind that protective wall she'd erected so carefully.

"I temporarily delayed the sheriff questioning you, but I can't protect you from his questions forever. Not unless I understand what's going on." Stefan leaned forward in his chair. "Give me the unvarnished truth, Faith. Did you take Zoe without her father's permission? Is that why you need to avoid the sheriff?"

Faith's head snapped to check on Zoe, obviously confirming that her daughter couldn't eavesdrop on their conversation. She crossed her arms in defiance. "Look, I'll never be able to thank you enough for saving Zoe, but I can't allow her anywhere near law enforcement. If that's not possible, take me to my car right now. We'll disappear and you can forget we ever met."

Her tone didn't leave room for negotiation and neither did the stubborn expression on her face.

"Forgetting about you isn't an option." He didn't

want to ask his next question, but he had to know. "Did your ex-husband hurt you? Did he hurt Zoe? Is that why you ran?"

"It's complicated." Faith twisted her fingers in her hands and touched the ring finger of her left hand. "He didn't hit me. Or Zoe. But he *is* dangerous."

Stefan studied her every microexpression, attempting to piece together her secret. He couldn't read her. What wasn't she telling him? "How dangerous? Would he kill Jerry or you?"

She didn't speak for a moment. "If I tell you, will you promise not to take us to the sheriff's office?"

Every instinct within Stefan urged him to agree. He hadn't survived the last decade without trusting his gut. "Agreed."

Her gaze bored into his, as if trying to gauge his honesty. He could tell her not to bother—he excelled at lying, yet another reason he was still alive. She didn't move for several moments. He dug into his pocket for the keys to his SUV and waited for the request to take them to the library to retrieve her car.

"I don't know how Burke found us," she said, chewing on her lip.

Her eyes darted back and forth. Stefan could almost see her mind playing out worst-case scenarios.

"We're in trouble," she finally admitted. Her leg bounced with nerves. "You saved Zoe's life, and I'm out of ideas."

"You can trust me."

"I hope so," she said with a long sigh. She sucked in a deep breath. "Zoe's name is flagged in the system.

The sheriff would have to send her to her father, and I can't allow that to happen."

At her admission, a silent curse slammed through Stefan's mind. "So this *is* about custody?"

"Not exactly." Faith rubbed her face. "I should start with Burke."

Finally. The moment she removed her hands from her eyes, Stefan nearly gasped aloud. He didn't think he'd ever forget her haunted expression so he simply waited, still and silent.

"I was so stupid to marry him," she bit out. "I wasn't good enough for him. Not thin enough, not blonde enough…just not enough. He divorced me and used Zoe to keep his parents happy. They want to make her into a little debutante. They can't see her for what she is."

He hadn't liked this guy from the moment he'd seen the fear on Faith's face, but her tone of defeat urged him to fold her into his arms and simply hold her. How could anyone believe Faith wasn't enough, that Zoe shouldn't be treasured?

"The last few months, Burke started laying groundwork to get full custody." Faith looked up at him with despair in her eyes. "I'm pretty sure someone called in false reports to Child Protective Services. They were at my door asking if I'd paid my bills for the month. When I reported Burke late on his child support they mumbled a few words, but nothing ever happened. Burke and his family have the money and the power. They want full custody. Someone like me can't fight them and win. I knew I could lose her. I was terrified."

"So you ran."

"I hadn't planned to." Faith rose and stared off into the desert. "I never wanted this."

"CTC has a lot of connections in the state and across the country. My team could help you fight your ex-husband's family. The right way."

She shook her head. "It's too late for that. A few months ago I would have jumped at the offer, but now—"

He joined her at the edge of camp. Gently, he turned her toward him. The fear in her eyes wasn't an act. Her ex-husband terrified her. Stefan placed his hands on her shoulders and squeezed lightly.

"What aren't you telling me, Faith?"

She averted her gaze from his.

"I'll wait for an answer as long as I have to." Stefan tilted her chin up with his finger. "I can help. If you'll just trust me."

She took a shuttering breath. "I haven't ever said it out loud. I still can't believe it."

"Tell me."

Conflict whirled behind her eyes. Finally, she swallowed.

Stefan didn't know what else he could do. What terrified her so much? Why couldn't he convince her to tell him?

Faith stared at him, still obviously struggling. She glanced at the tent and her brow furrowed. "Where's Zoe?" Frantically, she scanned the camp.

He followed her line of sight. "She can't have gone far."

"Zoe!" Faith called.

Stefan ducked his head into the tent. Not there. He perused the landscape, but the little girl had wandered out of sight. She couldn't have gone far. It had only been a few minutes.

His mind flashed to a horrifying possibility. "The creek," he shouted, racing toward the water.

"Is it deep?" Faith chased after him.

Before he could answer a horrified scream sounded through the desert air.

"Oww! Mommy! Mommy! Help me!"

They headed toward her voice and slid down the embankment. Zoe danced around, slapping her legs.

"What's wrong?" Faith shouted.

Stefan looked down. A swarm of red ants surrounded Zoe's feet.

"Fire ants." He grabbed Zoe and set her away from the nest she'd stumbled onto. Quickly, he flicked away the ones still crawling on her.

She cried out. "They hurt."

"I know," he said, scooping the lightweight into his arms. "I've got something that will help."

The little girl clung to his neck. Hard. For a tiny thing, she certainly had a grip.

"It hurts, Mommy. Hot prickly burns."

"I know, Slugger."

Stefan tightened his arms around her and ran back to the camp, Faith at his heels.

He passed a sobbing Zoe to her mother and knelt down in front of his cooler. Every cry twisted his heart a bit. "Where did they sting you?"

"My l-legs," she sobbed.

"Get her pants off," he ordered and dug into the chest for some ice.

Faith removed Zoe's pants, shoes and socks. Stefan crouched beside her and cleaned her legs with cool water and a bit of soap.

The moment the liquid touched Zoe, she sighed. "That feels better. I like the cool."

Red welts erupted on her legs. They had to hurt like hell. "They're fire ants. You can tell because they're reddish brown. They don't have an opening on the top of their nest so they fooled you. That's why you stepped on it."

Big tears slid down Zoe's cheeks. "I didn't mean to step on their house."

Stefan dug into his tent for a T-shirt and wrapped an ice-filled baggie inside. "Hold this on the welts. It should help. I'll get some cortisone cream."

Faith pressed the cold pack against Zoe's leg. She sucked in several shuddering breaths and leaned against her mother. Stefan returned with a small tube.

"Do you have the kitchen sink in that tent?" she asked.

"Necessities when you're living outside." He spread the cream on Zoe's feet, ankles and calves. "Did they get anywhere else?"

Her daughter wiped her eyes and shook her head.

"Okay, then. How about you go into my tent and we'll elevate your feet. Do you think you can do that?"

"What's elevate?"

"It means we'll put a pillow under them so they're above your heart. It'll help the swelling go down."

"The ants won't come inside the tent, will they?" Zoe asked, frowning at the ground in suspicion.

"We'll close the screen. You'll be safe."

Faith carried her daughter into the tent and settled her. She lay next to Zoe. The sound of Faith humming to her daughter filtered through the camp.

Fifteen minutes later, she sneaked out.

Crossing the camp, she grabbed her water bottle and plopped down across from him. "She's out, poor thing. Neither one of us slept well last night. Not after the house was ransacked."

She lifted her gaze to his, her eyes red and tired, her expression defeated. Stefan fought his instincts to push her. Sometimes stillness could extract the truth far more effectively than the most compelling persuasion. He longed to ask why, if her ex had the political upper hand, had Jerry torn through their things. Why had he tried to kidnap Zoe? It didn't make sense.

Instead, he waited.

Would he finally hear the truth she'd obviously kept to herself for quite a while?

Faith took a deep breath. "Burke has secrets."

Stefan nodded with encouragement.

"He killed someone," she rushed out. "In fact, he didn't murder just one person.

"My ex-husband is a serial killer."

Chapter Five

Burke paced the floor, his feet sinking deep into the carpet. A pile of unreviewed reports littered his desk. He'd been unable to focus since Orren had called. Damn Faith. She'd caused him more trouble than he'd thought possible.

Soon it would be over. If Orren could be trusted, within twenty-four hours she'd be dead. The thought didn't thrill him like it should have. He paused at his office's panoramic window and peered across the Dallas skyscape.

The room went hazy. An image of Faith appeared in the glass. His smiling, low-class, treacherous wife. Before his eyes, a stream of blood washed her away.

Burke shook his head and the vision dissipated. *He'd* wanted to be the one to make her disappear. He'd been dreaming about taking his favorite Bowie to her since she'd let herself go after Zoe had been born. Her hair no longer the perfect blond, she'd fattened up at least twenty pounds. She was no longer the trophy he'd molded from that waitress at the Shiny Penny.

She wasn't *his* Faith any longer. She'd forced him to divorce her.

Faith needed to be gone on *his* terms, not hers. And to discover she had some fool cowboy helping her. The very thought made Burke's head pound with each beat of his heart. He couldn't take it. He'd bet she'd given the guy her body. That she'd squealed underneath him like the low-class Jezebel she was. He just knew it. He might not want Faith anymore, but he damn sure didn't want anyone else to have what had belonged to him. He didn't share.

Burke grabbed his coat and walked out of his office, forcing his voice and demeanor to remain calm and controlled when inside he longed to scream. "I'm leaving for the day. Cancel my afternoon appointments."

Before his administrative assistant could ask him any questions, he walked into the elevator. The doors slid closed, leaving him in peaceful silence.

Finally alone.

Burke let out a loud curse. His ex had found herself another man. The guy must not have any class to want someone as broken down as Faith.

His body trembled, prickles of irritation flicked under his skin. He rubbed his arm until it turned red. It didn't help. Nothing would. He'd have to find a way to calm himself. His father wouldn't like it, but Burke was past caring.

He needed release. His bag was packed. His plan in place. The Acid Bath Murderer had always fascinated him. The original had been caught. Burke didn't plan to be.

Now all he needed was the right woman.

The elevator door slid open and he quickly blanked his expression even as he wanted to claw each inch of his body.

A woman stepped onto the elevator and acknowledged him with a nod. Her blond hair turned under just above her shoulders, sleek and smooth.

Polished.

Nothing like Faith.

He shoved his hands in his pockets, digging his thumbnails into his palms. Sometimes pain would drive the urge away for a while. He had rules he followed. One was not to hunt near where he worked or lived.

He glanced down at her hands. She wore a ring on the left one. She had someone else.

Blood pounded at the backs of his eyes. He closed them.

"Are you all right?" she asked in a husky voice that made his body harden in anticipation.

"Low blood sugar," he said, thinking quickly.

He loosened his hands. The pain dissipated. He'd made his choice.

Burke frowned and plastered a worried expression on his face. "I don't know if I should drive. Could you take me home?"

She looked at him, surprised. "I can call you a cab."

"Never mind. I'll find a way."

They exited the elevator at the parking garage level, and he stumbled through the doors.

She reached out to help him catch his balance.

He smiled up at her and plunged a syringe into her neck.

The shock on her face caused his body to pulse with pleasure, and he groaned at the release. He scooped her into his arms.

Sometimes rules were made to be broken.

Serial killer.

The desert horizon tilted. The campsite surrounding Faith faded away. The persistent trill of the cicadas drowned out the frantic beating of her heart. She pressed her fingers to her mouth. She'd said the words aloud for the first time since she'd called in an anonymous tip the night she and Zoe had left Weatherford.

As far as she could tell, nothing had come of her call. She couldn't be sure why, but it reinforced her decision as the right one. No one could stop Burke. He was untouchable.

Faith stared down at her hands before chancing a glance at Léon. She hadn't known him long. He'd been tough to read from the first time they'd met, but she recognized the surprise on his face.

Who wouldn't be shocked? Burke Thomas came from a wealthy family. He had money, good looks, and power. She'd run away for two reasons: no one would believe her, and she was terrified for Zoe.

Despite his promise, she half expected him to smile and cart her off to the sheriff—or maybe a psychiatrist's office.

His silence made her shoulders tense.

"How did you learn the truth about him?" he asked, brows drawn together.

Léon hadn't laughed in her face. He hadn't immediately dismissed her claims. In fact, he actually seemed to take her seriously.

"By chance." She twisted her hands in her lap, her nerves still jumping with dread. "He'd brought Zoe home after a weekend with him and her grandparents. Less than a half hour after he left, a lawyer delivered a new custody agreement." Faith couldn't stop the ironic chuckle from escaping her. "I'd hoped I could change his mind, so I tried to find him. My last stop was the bar where we'd met. I saw a prostitute getting into his car. Two days later, her photo appeared in the paper. She'd been murdered."

"It could have been a coincidence."

"That's what I tried to tell myself," she said with a frown. "For a while. A few weeks later, we argued about child support. He was behind again. I threatened to call his father. Two days afterward, the police found a body a couple counties over. The victim had blond hair and resembled the first woman, but she'd been killed in a completely different way."

Léon picked up a stick from the ground and poked at the cold ashes from the previous night's campfire. He didn't say anything for a moment. He thought she was insane. He had to.

"I know what you're thinking." She forced herself to stop fidgeting and met his thoughtful gaze. "I'm not crazy."

"Actually, I was waiting to hear what else you'd found. I have a feeling there's more."

For a moment she froze. Every time she'd pictured going to the cops—or anyone for that matter—she'd imagined being on the receiving end of condescending questions with an oh-so-reasonable tone that grated on her like a karaoke singer a half step off key. Léon's encouragement shattered the dam of silence.

The words, the thoughts held in confidence for so long, poured out. "I reviewed the newspapers, searching for murdered women. I found over a dozen tall, blonde, very thin women in the counties surrounding the Dallas-Fort Worth area. Almost all of the victims lived or were killed in different cities or towns. I recorded the dates. They all happened on days that Burke and I had a huge argument."

"You remember every argument?"

She bristled a bit. He didn't understand. Would he ever? Someone like him, who was clearly in control of his world. "I know which days Zoe stayed with Burke. When he brought her home, he pushed me. I pushed back."

Faith didn't mention how every encounter had ended with her dry heaving in the bathroom. Their arguments had upset Zoe, too. The love between her and Burke may have died, but she'd kept hoping they could both put their daughter's well-being first.

A scratching filtered through the air from the edge of the campsite. Léon shot to his feet and palmed his handgun. She'd never seen anyone move with such precision and economy of movement.

A prairie dog scurried at the edge of the campsite. He returned to his seat across from her and leaned forward. "You're convinced after each fight he walked out your door and committed murder?"

"I know it sounds crazy, but yes. That's exactly what I believe."

He rubbed his neck and the camp went silent for a few seconds. "Did you ever call the police?"

"I left an anonymous tip from a pay phone." She tucked one leg underneath her. "I couldn't think of anything else to do. The police knew about the custody battle. They'd come out several times on bogus calls—a tree branch crossing the property line, someone falsely reporting screaming. I'm pretty sure Burke called in as part of his plan to get full custody.

"I didn't think they'd believe me."

"Could you be wrong?" Léon propped the heel of his boot on the edge of a rock.

"I wanted to be wrong, but I'm not." Faith glanced over to make certain Zoe still slept and lowered her voice even further. "When we married, Burke tried to transform me to look like the women he killed."

Léon stilled, his eyes laced with incredulity. "Some might say a custody battle would be an excellent reason to suggest your ex is a murderer."

She didn't bother responding. Why should she? Instead, she retrieved a bag hidden beneath her things and dug out a thick expandable folder. "Maybe you'll believe this," she challenged.

Faith removed the rubber band holding her evidence in place. She passed over a newspaper clipping of the face of a blonde smiling into the camera. "The woman I saw Burke with outside a bar a few hours before she died." Faith pulled out an article she'd printed from the woman's social media site. The image still made Faith shiver. In color, the victim's hair was styled the way it had been that night, her dress designed to show off her prominent collarbones and very thin frame.

"Obviously the same woman."

His deep voice tugged Faith back to the present. "She was murdered on a Saturday night, the same night Burke and I argued. A few weeks later, Burke came over out of the blue. We had an arbitration scheduled about the custody agreement, but he wanted Zoe to stay with him all week. His father had some kind of event planned. I think Burke wanted to show Zoe off to his clients. I told him no. She had two baseball games she had to pitch. We had another fight. A couple of days later, I saw this article in the paper."

She passed the newspaper clipping, taking in every expression, every nuance as he read the article.

"There's a definite resemblance," he said, pointing at the grainy photo.

He met her gaze, and she followed the first two with another social media printout. Faith couldn't help but hold her breath. She'd never shown these documents to anyone.

Léon fingered through the items. "No doubt. They could be sisters." He returned the papers to her.

Faith clasped the evidence to her chest. "The photos made me nauseous. I think I must've known in that moment what was going on, but I didn't want to believe it."

His brow furrowed. "There's something you're not telling me."

He wouldn't understand until she showed him everything. Faith dug into the folder. "I went to the library and searched old papers." She slapped another woman's photo in his hand. "Two days after our divorce was final." Another photo. "Three days after he didn't receive sole managing conservatorship of Zoe, which is basically sole custody." She placed a stack of photos in his hands. "I found nine more. Every time I saw another photo I thought I was going to be sick."

Léon flipped through the pages. A low whistle escaped his lips. "Have the cops connected Burke? Surely they see the pattern?"

"I don't know." Faith shrugged. "There's been nothing in the paper. Maybe they're investigating after I called in my tip, but not one of these bodies was found in the same town. None of them were killed the same way. From what I've read, most serial killers have a pattern. Burke's pattern is that he *doesn't* have one."

She hesitated over the remaining two photos. Her skin tingled every time she stared at these images, but she handed them over anyway. "This is me."

Léon gripped the photos tight and fell back into his chair. She got that. When she'd first seen all the photos together, she'd sunk to the floor, unable to stand.

Faith knew exactly what he saw. Her, smiling, with a bone-thin figure hugged by the formfitting gown her husband had chosen, hair golden blond, piled on her head in an elegant chignon. She'd been Burke's image of perfection. He'd told her so. She'd been so happy;

she'd had no doubt she'd finally found her very own Prince Charming.

She'd found a monster disguised as a prince.

Léon studied the second picture of her poured into a skin-tight designer dress, her hair straight, with wisps of bangs. Faith winced at her emaciated body. She looked sick and starving.

"He chose my clothes. He dictated the cut and color of my hair." She let out a self-deprecating laugh. "He said it was because he wanted me to be the best I could be. That he wasn't trying to change me, just make me better. I believed him. I thought I was lucky he cared. For a while."

Léon tugged a cooler over to them and used it as a small table. He laid the photos down with Faith's picture in the middle. To Faith, the images shocked her as much now as the first time she'd seen them.

He let out a soft, low whistle. "You could *all* be sisters."

"And they're all dead." Faith met Léon's gaze. "Except me."

A SMALL BREEZE furled the photos spread out in front of Stefan. When he'd first met Faith, he'd assumed she'd been running from an abusive relationship, or someone showing a twisted interest in Zoe…anything but a man who was obviously murdering Faith over and over and over again in his twisted mind.

Crazy made it a tough capture. An organized psycho was easier to track due to their predictable nature. Burke seemed to be a very dangerous combination: an organized killer mimicking a disorganized one. The worst of the worst.

Faith sat across from him and chewed on her lips; a guarded expression settled in her eyes. She was waiting for his judgment, as if she feared he'd laugh at her.

"I'm impressed. I understand why no one identified the pattern. Until you." He couldn't give her enough credit. "If my company had compiled this package, we'd be on the cops' or district attorney's doorstep with high confidence the perpetrator wouldn't see the outside of a prison for the rest of his life. With all this—" he swept his hand across the pile of evidence "—why run?"

"Haven't you been listening?" Her voice grew urgent. "Burke and his family have too much influence. The Thomas family doesn't lose." Faith shook her head, the movements strong and emphatic. "I can't take the risk. I could *never* put Zoe in that kind of danger."

Her entire body shook. Stefan knelt in front of her, gripping her hands. He rubbed her ice-cold fingers between his. "You and Zoe are safe here."

"Because of you, but we can't live here forever." She didn't pull her hands away. "My plan to escape Burke is in the toilet. He found us in Carder, a town I'd never even heard of before my car broke down. How am I supposed to disappear without new identities for me and Zoe? He'll track us down. I just know it."

The despair in her voice struck his chest like a bayonet. More than that, he could see the loneliness in her, echoing his own.

CTC could help Faith. Ransom's contacts had to be

as influential as the Thomas family's. His challenge was, after fighting against power for so long, would Faith ever trust him enough to let them help?

He pulled her to her feet, determined to try. She stood stiffly. Ever so slowly, giving her ample opportunity to escape him, he trailed his hands up her arms to her shoulders and cupped her cheeks. His gaze held hers captive. "Listen to me, Faith. Whatever I have to do, however I have to do it, I'll make certain you and Zoe are safe. I promise you that. I think you should let me help get Burke the legal way, but if that fails, I have a friend. Her name is Annie. She can create new identities that Burke can never track. I promise."

"Really?"

He nodded.

She leaped at him and threw her arms around his neck in a grateful hug. He wrapped his arms around her, but within seconds, the warmth of her body tugged at him. He fought the instinct until she stilled. Faith cleared her throat and stepped out of his arms.

He couldn't speak. His gaze fell to her lips and he dragged his attention back to her eyes. Her pupils had dilated. Awareness sizzled between them.

She swallowed deeply and wet her lips.

Stefan nearly groaned in response. He shouldn't feel this way. He couldn't. He only had three days, though he'd already admitted to himself that however long it took, he'd see Faith and Zoe safe and secure before he carried out his own plans.

Faith gripped his shirt. She blinked once, then twice

and shook her head. "This can't happen," she whispered under her breath.

She stepped out of his embrace. Stefan let her go. She was so very right, but the moment she backed away, his heart chilled a few degrees.

He couldn't remember ever having such an intense reaction to a woman.

"I…umm… I think I'll rest," she said softly. "It's only three, but it's already been a very long day." She nodded at the tent where Zoe still slept.

He didn't say anything, and after one long look back at him, she ducked into the tent and zipped it closed.

Stefan let out a long sigh. Man, he was in more trouble than he'd thought.

He forced himself back to the makeshift table, familiarizing himself with every photo, every case file, everything Faith had compiled on her ex-husband. She might believe there was only one choice, but he would convince her to let CTC help. He'd run through every scenario.

He wouldn't risk Faith and Zoe to a madman.

By the time he raised his head, the afternoon sun beat down on the campsite. He stood and let out a long groan. He couldn't find a hole in her theory, and he was no lawyer, but her case wasn't a slam dunk. She'd fit together a plethora of damaging coincidences and the closest fact she had to a smoking gun was her own eyewitness testimony. A defense attorney would not only tear her apart, her discovery also placed a crosshair directly on her back.

Maybe she *should* run. Maybe he should call Annie

right now, except imagining Faith and Zoe looking over their shoulders for the rest of their lives didn't sit well. He understood the pitfalls all too well. No, he needed more time. There had to be a way to eliminate Burke as a threat.

After a last glance at the tent where his guests still slept, Stefan wandered over a couple of small dunes, through the shrub bush, until he was out of earshot. He dialed a familiar number on his sat phone.

"Sheriff's office," the dispatcher's voice answered.

"Blake Redmond, please."

"I'd recognize that smooth, mysterious accent anywhere. How are you, Mr. Royce?"

"Waiting for you to accept my proposal, Miss Iris."

She chuckled. "My husband of fifty-five years might not like that. The sheriff's pacing in his office cursing at the walls, I'd venture to say. That jerk he brought in for kidnapping that sweet girl ain't talking and Blake's spittin' mad. Hold while I connect you."

A click sounded through the earpiece.

"Redmond." The terse greeting didn't leave any doubt as to the sheriff's frustration.

"He won't talk, huh?" Stefan asked.

"You charm Iris out of that information?"

"Of course." He didn't have to tell Blake his dispatcher was also the town megaphone when it came to gossip.

"I should fire her, but she wormed her way in here after we lost Donna several years back. She's kind of like mold. Once she's there, she's tough to get rid of." A wooden creak indicating Blake sat in his chair filtered through the phone. "The guy's clammed up. I'm getting nowhere. I need to interview the girl and her mother."

"Look, Blake—" Stefan rubbed the base of his neck.

"Damn. I recognize the tone in your voice," the sheriff said in exasperation. "Let me guess. Things are worse than we thought, and she needs to hide and can't come into the station."

"You're good at this."

"No, I'm not, but every time I get involved with CTC I end up sitting back and doing nothing and the problem just vanishes. Am I going to uncover a bunch of dead bodies on that ranch someday?"

"I doubt it. Ransom doesn't leave evidence."

A long sigh escaped from Blake. "I know you guys help people I can't, but it gets old."

"You could always join up. There might be an opening soon." Stefan deliberately allowed his words to reveal more than he usually did.

Blake didn't respond for a few seconds. "You thinking about leaving?"

"Let's just say it's time for a change."

"I'm happy with my family and my life here, thank you very much. Why don't you quit trying to veer me off my target? What's going on?"

"You'd be a good operative," Stefan acknowledged. He kneaded the back of his neck. "Between you and me, her ex is searching for her, and he doesn't wear a white hat."

"Sheriff!" Iris's voice squealed through the phone. "Come quick."

"What the hell?" A wooden crash erupted through the phone. "I'll call you back."

The phone went silent.

Stefan waited for a few moments, but when Blake didn't immediately get in touch with him, he made his way back to the campsite. He'd try again later. Hopefully the emergency had nothing to do with Stefan's witness, but he had a bad feeling.

His footsteps soundless, Stefan crossed to the pile of evidence and took out the wedding photo of Burke Thomas and Faith. The man oozed charm and an easy smile. Of course, so had Ted Bundy.

"That's my daddy when he was nice to my mom," Zoe said from his side.

Stefan jerked in surprise. He quickly shoved the other photos into Faith's folder. The kid was light on her feet. Or he had already become too comfortable with his guests. Both possibilities disconcerted him.

He forced his shoulders to relax. "You'd make a good spy, Zoe."

"Thanks." She grinned. "Is that what you are, a spy?"

Stefan looked down at her, her face so open and eager. Strangely, he found himself not wanting to lie to her. "I guess you could say that."

"Really?" Her eyes gleamed with excitement. "Like in the movies?"

"Well, investigating isn't as exciting as in the movies." Okay, that was a half-truth. He'd been tortured in a dungeon, almost blown up on more than one occasion, nearly outed during several undercover ops and forced to play long-range sniper to save the lives of his CTC teammates. "Mostly I read a lot and figure stuff out. Kind of like homework."

Zoe wrinkled her nose. "That doesn't sound like fun."

"Catching a bad guy and sending him to jail is fun."

Her eyes cleared. "That's good. Bad people should be in jail so they can't hurt good people."

"Exactly right." Stefan knelt to face her eye to eye. "Are you feeling better?"

"I've got little white bumps where the ants bit me." She lifted her pants leg and showed him. "They're itchy."

"How about we use some more medicine?"

"Okay." Zoe nodded and plopped in the chair across from Stefan.

She lifted her legs, and he rubbed the cortisone cream onto her ankles and calves.

"Thanks. You know how to put on medicine real good. Do you have kids?"

That all-too-familiar pang of regret twisted inside his chest. "I have two nieces and a nephew. In fact, my niece and nephew are twins. They're about your age."

"Could I play with them?" Zoe practically bounced in her seat. "Are they nearby?"

"I wish they were, kiddo. They live across the ocean." He rubbed the last inflamed spot and pulled her pants legs down.

"Do you fly on a plane to visit them?"

"Not as much as I'd like." Now there was an understatement. "Sometimes families are complicated."

"What's com...pli...cated?"

That had Stefan stumped. "Confusing," he settled on. "Sometimes we don't get to do what we want to do because it's hard to figure out the right thing to do."

Okay, that didn't make a whole lot of sense to him, but Zoe nodded her head.

"Yeah, I understand. My life is complicated, too. My daddy likes me to wear dresses with lace. I like jeans and T-shirts. But since my grandma gets me the dresses as a present, I gotta wear them. It's hard."

Stefan chuckled at the horrified expression on the little girl's face. "You don't like frilly dresses?"

"They get in the way. You can't play baseball in a dress. It'll get dirty and then you get yelled at." She swung her feet back and forth. "If I didn't have to wear a dress, I'd like to go on a plane with my dad. He promised to take me, but he's really busy. Did your daddy take you on a plane?"

So that was another very complicated question Stefan wasn't quite sure how to answer. The good memories of his childhood had been overtaken by a devastating truth. He couldn't imagine his father would have been part of the plot that had cost Stefan's brother his life, and Stefan his freedom. He wished Zoe would never have to deal with the same disillusionment, but she would learn her father's identity someday. He hadn't actually asked, but Faith's behavior and Zoe's actions had made it clear the little girl knew nothing about her father.

The phone interrupted them. He glanced at the

screen. Not a number he recognized. "Zoe, stay here. I'll be right back."

He walked out of the girl's earshot. "Léon Royce."

"It's hit the fan here," Blake said. "My prisoner keeled over dead, and I don't know how."

"Heart attack?"

"He's young for that. Maybe he took a pill or poisoned himself, but I can't tell. One visitor who used a fake name, but that was hours ago. I called the medical examiner in from Odessa. We'll know soon enough."

"Damn it," Stefan said. "I was hoping he could confirm Faith's story."

"Well, he's not talking now. On the other hand, I have some surprising news for you. I just received a call pretty high up in the state attorney general's office. They want me to verify the identity of my kidnap victim as a seven-year-old girl named Zoe Thomas. But get this, I'm supposed to keep it on the down low if I find her, and just get back to *him*, and no one else. Of course, the guy included a not-so-subtle threat to audit my budget and the past five years of cases if I don't cooperate."

Stefan let out a low whistle. If he'd needed proof to support Faith's story, Blake had just given him solid testimony of the power of Faith's ex-husband.

"Her ex is tipping his hand. Why?"

"I don't know, but I don't like being pushed around. I sure as hell don't like a prisoner dying on me."

"This entire situation's uglier than I expected," Stefan admitted.

"It's a cover-up of a different kind, that's for sure."

Blake's voice lowered. "I called on a burner phone, and I didn't say this to you, but don't call me back. I don't know where you are and I don't want to know. Whoever's after that little girl has some powerful friends. I'd stay as far away from the law as you can."

Chapter Six

Something hard and pointed pressed into Faith's lower back. She lay still and rubbed her eyes. For a moment, she didn't know where she was.

A breeze blew across her face and she opened her eyes to the view of the top of Léon's tent.

Léon.

Zoe.

She snapped her gaze to the empty space next to her and shot to a sitting position. A rock ground into her hip, but she ignored the pinch. She vaulted out of the tent and lifted her hand against the late-afternoon sky.

The bright sun beat down, heating her face. She winced at the glare and crinkled her eyes to search the campsite.

Léon and Zoe were both gone.

Faith's heart seized in panic until joyful laughter wafted from somewhere behind the tent. When had she last witnessed true happiness in her daughter's voice? A pang of guilt weighted down Faith's shoulders. Zoe deserved so much more than what Faith could give her right now.

Homeless, on the run, without a plan. What kind of mother was she?

Zoe erupted in another trill of laughter. Faith trudged toward the noise, tracking the sound to the creek. The sight made her pause.

Léon hovered near Zoe, pointing at the ground. She crouched and looked up at their rescuer, unadulterated adoration painted on her face.

Faith's heart melted. Who wouldn't be enamored with the man who had saved her life, and in this moment treated her as if she were the most important person in the world?

He'd made Faith feel that way when she'd very nearly fallen into his arms. He'd believed her when she'd thought no one would. He'd offered to help, and he'd promised to find a way for Zoe and her to be safe.

Faith's head might doubt, but her gut actually trusted him.

Léon smiled at Zoe and softly patted her cheek. The gentle movement caused Faith's heart to flip in her chest. If she let herself, she could fall for him, too.

Scooching behind a rock, she peeked out to watch them. She needn't have bothered to attempt to be inconspicuous. From a side view, Léon gave Faith a quick wink before focusing on her daughter.

"You know a lot about camping." Zoe perched on a rock by the stream. "Can I tell you something?" Her daughter's voice had turned serious.

Faith strained to hear.

"Sure." Léon knelt in front of Zoe. "Is something wrong?"

"I got lost today." Zoe bowed her head. "I stepped

on the ants because I didn't know which way to go. I was scared."

Faith eased out from her hiding place, ready to comfort her daughter, but the tender expression on Léon's face made her pause.

He pushed his hat back and met Zoe's gaze, unblinking and serious. "It's okay to be scared. Everyone is afraid sometimes."

"Well, I didn't like it." Zoe crossed her arms and took a stubborn stance Faith recognized all too well. "I didn't know what to do. What if I hadn't yelled? I might have gone the wrong way and lost you and Mom. I can barely see the camp from here."

"Hmm." Léon stroked his chin. "Well, I camp out a lot, and I know the rules for getting lost. Want to hear them?"

Zoe's eyes widened a bit and she nodded, giving Léon her devoted attention.

"Okay." He held out his hand and Zoe grabbed it. He led her a few feet from the edge of the creek. "First, you stay on a trail, like this one." He pointed to a path in the dirt. "Animals made this to drink water. If I'm looking for you, I'll go down all the trails first to find you."

"What if there's not a trail?"

"You find a place out of the cold and wind, like over by those rocks, and wait for me and your mom to find you. And whatever you do, don't wander around at night. There are no streetlights when you're camping."

"What if you don't see me?" Zoe asked, her forehead furrowed with worry.

"That's where your orange backpack comes in."

Léon grinned. "Put it outside wherever you're hiding. It's so bright, I'll be able to see it. And while you're waiting, make a lot of noise as often as you can."

Zoe took all the information in, then frowned. "But what if I'm hiding from bad people? Mom always says to stay quiet. What do I do then?"

Faith's heart broke at the question. Zoe shouldn't have those thoughts.

"Good point." Léon paused for a moment, as if trying to form his answer. "You leave me a sign that I can follow."

"What kind of sign?"

"Well, I'd recognize one of your shoelaces, or even a pen or pencil from your bag. I'd know it's you, and since we've had this talk, I'd know where to look." He clasped her daughter's shoulders. "I'd find you, Zoe. I promise."

She bit her lip, scanning the trail over to the rock before finally nodding her head. "I think I can do that. Thanks, Léon."

"We're not done yet," he said. "Which direction are we facing right now? North, south, east or west?"

She pursed her lips and twisted her mouth. Faith recognized the face. Zoe shared it often enough while doing her homework when she wasn't quite certain of the answer.

"Take your time," he said, scratching the dirt with a stick. "You don't have to panic. Just be logical. Where's the sun right now?"

Zoe's eyes brightened. She pointed in the sky. "You told me the sun rises in the east and sets in the west.

That way's west, so…" She knelt and dragged her finger through the dirt. "We're facing north."

"Excellent." Léon smiled and lifted his hand. Zoe slapped him a high five. "When you know which way you're headed, you won't go in circles if you're lost."

Her daughter sighed, loud and long. "There's a lot to remember about getting lost." She peeked up at Léon.

"Then how about we practice? I'll go over to that rock." He pointed to Faith's hiding place. "You pretend you're lost and figure out what to do."

"Like a game." She scampered off.

Léon walked over to Faith and met her behind the rock.

"Survival 101?" she asked.

He shrugged. "It was something to do."

"It was more than that," Faith said. "Thank you for helping her not be afraid." She leaned back against the boulder, one eye on Zoe's adventure. "Do you like living this way? In the middle of nowhere?"

"I miss a hot shower on occasion. I have a system jury-rigged, but it's nothing compared to high-pressure water pounding on your back. Other than that, yeah, I like the silence. How it gets totally dark and I can see all the stars in the sky." Stefan propped himself beside her. "What are you thinking?"

"I'm wondering if I could live like this with Zoe for a while. Just until I can figure out what to do next."

"You can stay as long as you need to," he offered.

Faith's entire body relaxed. At least she didn't have to worry about shelter or food. Today anyway. "Thank you. You're saving our lives."

His gaze shifted away, almost as if he were embarrassed. "Zoe," he called out. "I'm coming to find you."

They rounded the large rock. Faith scanned the area. Zoe was gone. "Where is she?"

"Don't worry. I haven't let her out of my sight. She's testing me. She wants to make certain I really will find her." Léon glanced at the ground. "We follow the trail." He held out his hand. "Come on."

Faith linked her fingers with his. They wandered down by the creek to a narrow dirt path.

"It's a sheep trail. Livestock graze on both public and private land out here."

They picked their way among the shrub bushes to the rocky outcropping. Right next to a large boulder, in plain sight, Zoe's backpack gleamed in the afternoon sun.

"Help!" a voice cried out. "I'm here."

They raced over to the rock. Zoe sat grinning in a small indentation.

Léon gave her a second high five. "Great job. You'd be out of the wind and rain if you hid in this little hole."

Zoe looked at Léon. "Well?" she asked, her hands on her hips, an eager expression of expectation on her face.

He made a show of hemming and hawing and finally sighed. "Okay, I guess you've earned it."

"What's going on with you two?" Faith asked, biting her cheek to keep from smiling at their antics.

Léon placed something in Zoe's hand. She ran over to her mother. "Look. A little flashlight to keep with me. And an arrowhead. Léon found it near the creek. I earned them for doing a good job."

Faith hugged her daughter. *Thank you*, she mouthed over her daughter's head.

A slight flush tinged his cheeks and he glanced at his watch. "Are you hungry?"

"I am," Zoe shouted out. "We missed lunch and we're out of peanut butter."

"I think we may do a little better than peanut butter." He led them back to the fire pit and dug into a sealed cooler. "Salmon okay?" he asked.

"You've got to be kidding." Faith's mouth fell open.

"I may live out in the middle of nowhere, but I like a good meal at the end of the day." He adjusted the rocks surrounding the ash-laden hole in the ground.

"Can I help?" Zoe asked.

"Sure. First I have to build a fire."

Zoe's eager expression made Faith want to wince. One look at her face and Léon sent her a stern look. "No fire-starting without an adult. Do you understand, Zoe?"

Much to Faith's relief, her daughter nodded and hunkered down beside him. Faith pulled one of the chairs closer to the pit. She studied Zoe's awestruck expression as she hung on Léon's every word. He pointed out the magnesium fire starter; he showed her what grass made good tinder and how to pick out small, dry sticks for kindling, and even how a half-gutted log would help the fire grow at first. Within a few minutes, the flames gleamed brightly.

He pulled out foil, some corn ears and asparagus, a grill and two iron skillets, and a bag of what looked like cooked apples, and quickly threw a meal together.

"You come prepared."

"Necessity breeds skill."

As their dinner cooked, Léon poked at the blaze. "So, Zoe. Another quiz. If I walked toward the sun for a whole hour, how would I get back here?"

"Is this a trick question?" she asked.

"Nope. What do you think?"

Zoe stood up and started walking a few paces. She turned around to look at them. "You go backward," she said with a triumphant smile. "You walk the same time with the sun behind you."

"You're a definite pro," he said with a grin.

"What if there's no sun?"

"Then you can find a special star and do the same thing."

"Will you show me?"

"When it gets dark."

"I like it here with you, Léon. Can we stay?"

"As long as you want," he said quietly, sending Faith a sidelong glance. She shivered under his stare. She couldn't deny the attraction between them. She hadn't expected it, and could only see trouble if she gave into the feelings, but it was there just the same.

He clearly felt it, too. He strode over to her. "You okay?"

What was she supposed to say? She cleared her throat. "I appreciate everything you're doing for Zoe. You've made her feel safe for the first time in months."

"She's a great kid."

Faith cleared her throat. "You've let us horn in on your privacy when you didn't have to. I don't know what to say, how to…" Her voice trailed off and with a tentative touch, she reached for his hand. She wasn't sure why. He didn't pull away. Her heart skipped a beat. Faith raised her gaze to his. She recognized the awareness, the heat in his eyes. Another time, another place, she would lean into him and let him hold her all night long.

Zoe raced up between them, destroying the moment. "Is dinner ready yet?" she asked. "I'm hungry."

Faith cleared her throat and turned to her daughter, shoving back her own desires.

Léon stood statue still and studied her with that inscrutable expression she'd come to recognize. What was he thinking? Did he want to hold her as much as she wanted him to? Even though she shouldn't.

"Dinner's not quite done, but soon. I need to gather some more firewood and make a call," Léon said. "I'll be back."

Before Zoe could offer to go with him he disappeared behind a small hill.

Faith dropped her head in her hands.

"Mom? Are you okay? Your face looks hot."

She forced herself to look at her daughter. "I'm fine, sweetie. Just figuring out where we're going to go next."

"Since that bad guy's in jail, can we go home? Then can I call Danny? There's a new coach for baseball, and I have to try out again."

"I'm sorry, sweetie…" The impact of Zoe's words hit Faith. "How do you know about the new coach?"

She grasped Zoe's arms, but her daughter glanced away.

"Zoe? Have you been in contact with Danny?"

She swallowed. "I know I wasn't s'posed to, but I… I sent him a video message from the library computer."

Faith froze. "D-did you contact your father?"

Zoe dug her shoe into the dirt. "I…I thought about it."

"Did you?" Faith held her breath. "I'm not going to be mad, Zoe, but I need to know."

"I didn't, Mom. I promise."

Somehow Burke had traced the message Zoe had sent to her best friend. That was how he'd found her in Carder. Faith hadn't even known Burke knew about Danny.

Her knees buckled and she fell into the chair behind her. "Zoe, I know it's hard for you to understand, but it's important your father doesn't know where we are. Not yet."

"Because Daddy wants me to live with him?"

The words skewed Faith's gut. "How do you know that?"

Her daughter refused to meet her gaze. "I'm not s'posed to talk about what I hear by accident. You said so."

She clasped Zoe's shoulders. "This is important. Tell me, Slugger."

Her daughter scuffed her toe in the dirt. "One time I heard him tell Grandpa that if you were in an accident, I could go be with them forever."

THE THOMAS FAMILY's palatial estate stood well off the main road in the exclusive neighborhood of Preston Hollow. Burke strode up to his parents' home, livid.

He'd never been more embarrassed in his entire life than when the waitress at the most exclusive restaurant in all of Dallas had refused to return his credit card. He couldn't believe his father's audacity.

The butler answered the door. "Good evening, Mr. Burke."

"Where is he?" Burke asked.

"His study." The butler cleared his throat. "He's not in a good mood."

"Neither am I."

Burke stalked into his father's domain. When he was a child, he'd never been allowed inside. Sometimes entering the dark, mahogany-lined room made him feel like a ten-year-old kid.

Of course, his father treated him like one.

"You cut off the money," he said, slamming the door closed.

His father leaned back in his chair. "You didn't control your urges, did you? And this time you picked someone from *my* company. The whole place is freaked out. I had to bring in a damned psychologist for grief counseling. Do you know how much productivity you've cost me? And all because you couldn't keep your hands off that woman."

The vein on the side of his father's temple bulged; his mouth tightened. Burke hadn't seen him so upset in a long time. He narrowed his gaze. "Did you know her?"

His father's cheeks flushed.

Burke recognized the guilty expression. "Unbelievable. You were sleeping with her." He crossed the room and poured two fingers of Scotch. "I should've known. She's your type." He downed the shot in one large gulp. "Does Mom know?"

His father bristled. "She doesn't need to. I give your mother what she requires of me. Always have."

At the words, Burke rushed across the room and grabbed his father by the throat. "You betray her every day."

His father shoved him away. "And what do you think she'd do if she learned that her precious son is a murderer?"

Burke found his footing and glared at his father. "You wouldn't."

"Don't push me, son. I could stop protecting you and send a very informative envelope of evidence, complete with photographs and video, to the district attorney."

Burke dug his fingernails into his palms.

"That's right. I caught you on videotape. And I'll use it."

This couldn't be happening. Burke stared down at the floor. His father had to be bluffing.

"Don't worry. It's safe. The camera equipment was damaged…somehow."

Burke's head jerked up. What was his old man playing at? His father had threatened more than once to hold Burke's *hobby* over his head. He'd gone so far as drafting commitment papers, though he doubted the old man would ever use them. If he did, the world would learn too many secrets about the Thomas family, and his father couldn't have that.

Burke glared at his father; the veneer of civility had vanished. "What do you want?"

"Control yourself and get my granddaughter back permanently so she's no longer poisoned by her low-class mother. Can you do those two simple things, or do I have to take care of you like always?"

"I'm dealing with Faith. You'll have Zoe back soon."

"And the other?"

"Fine. I'll find another outlet for my…urges. You happy?"

His father sighed, that disappointed sigh that made Burke's belly burn with resentment.

"I'll have to be. Your mother only gave me an heir, not a spare."

Burke spun on his heel and stumbled on the carpet. The barb shouldn't have fazed him, but instead had made him appear vulnerable. He dug his fingernails into his palms again so hard a bead of sweat popped on his forehead. He straightened his back and strode across the room, careful with each step.

"Burke, don't screw up again. You'll find me to be a difficult enemy."

So am I, old man. So am I.

THE GENTLE COOS of quail pulled Faith out of a death-like night's sleep. Zoe slept curled next to her mother, co-cooned in Léon's tent. Even though they had no walls, no solid door and no alarm, Faith felt safe.

She liked the feeling.

Easing away from Zoe, Faith stretched her arms and shoulders. Keeping her movements as silent as possible, she quietly drew down the tent's zipper and peered outside.

Dawn peeked over the horizon, with brilliant purple and orange and pink meshing in a kaleidoscope of color.

One thing about sunrises in the desert, they really couldn't be topped. The scent of coffee wafted over to her. She rubbed her eyes and a figure in black, loose-fitting pants that rode low on his hips and no shirt made her freeze.

Léon shifted his foot forward, his movements deliberate and practiced. He threw a series of vertical punches, his arms straining, muscles quivering. He drew in a deep controlled breath and executed two complex sliding kicks before finally bringing his hands slowly together.

She'd never witnessed anything quite so beautiful. He controlled every movement with precision. His chest was dusted with hair and gleamed with sweat. Her belly quivered in response.

Since falling for Burke she'd been turned off by a pretty face, but Léon made her rethink that position.

His body relaxed and he blew out a long, slow breath. He adjusted his stance and turned away from her. She gasped. His back was covered in scars. They crisscrossed all over. Several long, thick discolorations appeared near his kidneys and they disappeared below his waistline.

He whirled around, cursed and grabbed his T-shirt, yanking it on.

They couldn't pretend she hadn't seen them.

"Coffee?" he asked, walking over to the fire as if nothing had happened.

"Sure." What was she supposed to say?

He handed her the cup. She looked down. "Do you have sugar?"

In silence, he opened a tub and pulled out several packets. She dumped one in and stirred.

She stared at the swirling dark brown liquid.

"I was captured. It happened a long time ago," he finally said. "My own choices led to my predicament." Léon shrugged. "Part of my old job. My previous life."

She lifted her gaze. She blinked slightly to clear the emotion from her eyes. "I'm sorry."

"I survived. I have a new life now. It's over."

His words closed that conversation, but Faith let his statement reverberate in her mind. The warmth of the cup filtered through to her hand, but it didn't touch the chill that had settled around her gut. "I've been thinking a lot about my future." She held the warm cup in her hands. "Tell me more about Annie."

That she'd brushed aside the idea that he and CTC could help her stung. "Are you sure?"

"I don't want to run. I want Burke to pay for what he's done, but I can't trust the system. It's stacked against us." She raised her gaze to his. "I don't have a choice."

He sat beside her. "Your past will follow you. If not physically, emotionally. The question is, can you live in the present? Your new present? Without wishing for what might have been?" He took her hand in his. "It won't be easy with Zoe. She's old enough to remember, but not old enough for you to be sure she can keep this secret. She'll have to get used to a new name, a new place. She won't be able to tell anyone about her past."

His words vibrated with truth…and with firsthand knowledge. She searched his gaze. "You've found a new life, haven't you? You have friends, people who care about you? People you count on?"

Léon didn't speak for a moment.

"Haven't you?" she asked again.

He cleared his throat. "Do you have family besides Zoe?"

She didn't like that he refused to answer the question. Maybe she'd assumed too much. "My folks died when I was twenty," she said. "Right before I met Burke. I have some cousins, but we never saw them. They live back east. Vermont, or maybe New Hampshire."

"That will make the transition easier. A new identity won't weigh on you as much." Léon sighed. "Annie's a pro. I ought to know. She can help you and Zoe disappear. As long as you follow her rules, you'll be okay. And safe."

"Will the $10,000 I have be enough?" Faith had a feeling Annie's services were much more valuable than anything Ray had offered.

"She owes me a favor. It'll be enough. And you don't have a choice, Faith."

"And you know she's the best." Faith shifted in her chair. "Is Léon your real name?"

He tilted his head. "What do you think?"

She studied his closed-off expression. "You know

too much about what Annie can do for us. Besides, I've never thought Léon fit you somehow."

"You're smart, and beautiful and very intuitive." He cupped her face in his hand, holding her captive with his gaze. "I don't let people see through me often. I don't know what it is about you."

She leaned in closer to him. "This isn't a good idea. I'm leaving."

"I know. Which is why I'm not fighting the temptation."

He lowered his mouth to hers, exploring her with a kiss that was gentle and powerful at the same time.

Faith shivered under the touch of his lips. He didn't press her body close. He held her face between his hands and his lips and tongue seduced her.

She couldn't have stood if she'd wanted to. She finally knew what the phrase *legs feeling like jelly* meant.

He raised his head and looked deep into her eyes. "That was…surprising."

The moment his lips left hers, a strange coldness invaded her. She hoped her mouth wasn't hanging open in shock. Her heart raced, thudding against her chest. Her entire body trembled. She gripped his collar. "Don't stop."

Faith pulled him back to her. With a groan, he wrapped his arms around her, pressing her tight against him. His kiss wasn't gentle this time. But neither was hers. He demanded. She wanted.

The flames licked at her very soul. She couldn't stop touching him. Her hands worked their way beneath his shirt, and she pushed it up. He lifted his mouth just long enough to let her toss his T-shirt away. She explored every inch of skin. His body was hard and firm. His back marred with scars. He sucked in a breath.

He'd been through so much, and he hadn't hesitated to help her, to protect her. To save Zoe.

The worry and fear disappeared with the touch of his hand on the bare skin of her back. She couldn't catch her breath. She'd never wanted anyone the way she wanted him.

She didn't know his real name, but she knew enough to know she trusted him.

Suddenly, he lifted his head. His heart thudded against her palm. She took a shuddering breath.

Before she could ask why he'd stopped, a soft buzzing sound filtered through her fuzzy brain.

The noise got louder, closer. He stared up into the sky and let out a curse. "A drone."

He grabbed her hand. "Head for cover. Now." He dragged her to the tent and they ducked inside.

Zoe shot up, immediately awake. "What's wrong?"

Faith pulled Zoe toward her, pressing the little girl close.

Léon crouched inside the tent and peered out. The buzzing swooped down closer. The drone flew over them, then circled in for another pass.

Faith's heart slammed against her ribs. She could barely process what was going on.

Had Burke found them again? She had no other explanation. This was why they had to run, why they needed new names. If only she could make Zoe understand they truly had to disappear. Forever.

Otherwise, they'd never be free. He'd always find them.

She looked over at Léon, not caring if he saw her fear.

His jaw tightened. "Someone's found us."

Chapter Seven

The morning sky offered no clouds, no cover. The drone had pinned them down. Stefan shoved his hand through his hair and peered through the tent's mesh screen.

"It's Burke, isn't it?" Faith's face had paled to the color of milk.

He wished he could reassure her, but he didn't know. Besides, whether it was her ex or Ray's contacts or even Stefan's enemies, it didn't matter. They'd been compromised.

All he could do now was minimize their vulnerabilities. Most drones recorded their information on an SD card and didn't necessarily go wireless. Either way, the machine had captured too many images, including Faith and Zoe, Stefan's face, the scars on his back and their license plate. If there was a chance he could keep the images and location from being disseminated, he had to take it. Hell of a shot, though, given the speed.

"You two stay here," he ordered.

Keeping his head low, he raced to his truck, dug into the cab and pulled out his rifle case. Within seconds he'd yanked open the zipper and lifted the Keppeler KS-V. His obligatory stint in his country's military had highlighted his unusual skill at long-distance shooting. It'd been the reason CTC had approached him for covert operations in the first place.

The drone made yet another pass over the camp, its camera visible at the bottom of the machine. He pressed the butt of the weapon to his bare shoulder and swept the barrel toward the drone. Whoever flew the machine may have recorded the location of the camp, but if they hadn't written it down or if they were counting on the drone's memory to keep the info, Stefan might be able to buy them some time.

He'd just have to hope the footage wasn't being recorded remotely.

Stefan sighted the drone and estimated the speed. He couldn't hesitate, not while his target kept on a steady path. He lined up the target, and anticipating its speed and trajectory, took in a slow breath. His instincts took over. He exhaled, and in between heartbeats, squeezed the trigger.

The loud crack echoed across the landscape. The drone broke apart in midair, its remains plummeting onto the desert floor several hundred feet to the south.

He swept his weapon along the landscape in a circle, searching for any vehicles. Nothing for at least twenty miles in any direction. He had a few minutes, but they couldn't hang around long.

"You can come out now," he called. He grabbed his T-shirt from the ground and tugged it on.

Zoe barreled out of the tent and raced to him. "You shot it? Right out of the sky?" Her eyes shone with awe.

"It's one of my jobs." Stefan returned his rifle to the case and met Faith's gaze over the girl's head. "We're leaving in ten minutes. Pack your things as fast as you can."

"Zoe," Faith said, nodding her head toward the tent. "Go ahead. I'll be right there."

Surprisingly, Zoe didn't argue or resist. Maybe it was the flat order from Faith, or the urgent tone in her mother's voice. Whatever the reason, the little girl raced to the tent while Faith followed Stefan out of the camp.

"Where are you going?" she asked, hurrying to his side.

"To check the camera and retrieve any memory chips that could identify us or the vehicle."

She paled and clutched his arm. "Are you telling me Burke may have *seen* us?"

"If it was Burke at all. The drone may not be your husband's. It could be Ray or the men he hasn't paid for your ID. Or, as you may have inferred, I have my own set of enemies." Stefan glanced over his shoulder. Zoe had set her knapsack outside the tent.

"You don't really believe that, do you?" She matched him step for step. "After everything, I don't need to be placated, Léon."

He scowled at her use of his alias. Before they parted he'd really like for her to call him by his given name. Just once. Strange how badly he wanted what he'd never wished for in the past.

Stepping up his pace, he picked through a thick group of shrub bushes. "I think chances are better than even that your husband is using some rather extraordinary means to find you and Zoe."

He knelt beside a twisted mess of plastic and metal. The drone hadn't been military quality. He popped out the hard drive and SD card and filtered through more wreckage. He let out a curse. The transmitter was expensive. He took a series of quick photos with his phone. "I can't tell if the video could live-stream ten miles out. I'll find out. Either way, they know our coordinates, so we're out of time."

They rushed back to the campsite. Zoe had taken it upon herself to pack up her mother's duffel and she'd even placed Stefan's makeshift kitchen items in a box.

"Are you sure you're not twenty instead of seven?" Stefan kept his tone joking and light, but even as he said the words he grabbed the duffel and box she'd packed and shoved them into the back of his SUV.

She poked her chest out and placed her hands on her hips. "I'm a big help. Just ask Mom."

Faith knelt and hugged Zoe. "I don't know what I'd do without you, Slugger." She rose and looked around the campsite. "Let's load everything into Léon's truck. I'll race you."

Zoe chuckled and they darted around the area, folding up camp chairs and putting away his kitchen staples. Faith laughed with her daughter, but Stefan recognized the tension lining her mouth, the stiffness in her back and shoulders.

Nothing could be done about that. Except to get them to safety.

They disappeared into the tent once more. The moment they began talking, Stefan grabbed his sat phone and called a number he rarely dialed.

The phone rang once, twice, three times. What if Daniel wasn't home?

A click sounded.

"Stefan?" Daniel Adams asked, his tone surprised. Maybe even shocked. "Is that you?"

For a moment Stefan simply closed his eyes. Daniel was the only person to use his given name these days. The man who had saved his life daily for weeks.

"How's your family?" Stefan tucked in his earpiece and pocketed the phone so he could finish loading the SUV. He shoved several tubs filled with tracking equipment and weapons and moved on to the boxes Zoe and Faith and closed.

"Unbelievable. The girls are into everything, and Hope's still in remission. We're going on almost four years now. I think we've beat it. Knock on wood."

"That's terrific." Stefan grabbed a bag of tools and the camp chairs, stowing them away. "How are the flashbacks?"

The last time he'd communicated with Daniel, his friend had still been struggling, though he'd improved a thousandfold since he'd vanished from a VA hospital and walked across the country to clear his head. Of course, he'd met his wife, fallen in love and found a family in the process. Not to mention all the headwork.

Daniel didn't answer for a moment. "Under con-

trol. I doubt they'll ever go away but I'm managing."
He paused. "Are you having them?" his friend asked
quietly. "Is that why you called?"

Only Daniel knew what had really happened to Stefan in the dungeon. Stefan had spent months in the hidden catacombs below his family's castle in the small
country of Bellevaux. He'd expected to die, but the
handoff to the terrorist leader who'd paid for the priv-
ilege had been delayed. Stefan's brother-in-law-to-be
and a few others from CTC had rescued them before
the exchange could be made.

"Sleeping outside helps," Stefan said. "Seems to me
you gave me that advice."

"A bed isn't a bad way to spend the night. You
should try it, my friend."

The sound of soft footsteps coming up behind him
caused Stefan to pause. Faith cleared her throat.

"Hold on, Daniel," Stefan said. He faced Faith. "If
I take down the tent, can you fold it up while I get the
rest?"

"Sure." She set down two more bags. "That's the
last of it."

Stefan glanced at his watch. "I'm back, Daniel."

"Distracted by a lovely female voice. Sounds like
your life is improving," Daniel said with a smile in his
voice. "So why this phone call out of the blue?"

"I need a favor." He loaded the last two bags and
quickly toured the area.

"Anything for you, Stefan. You know that."

"You may change your mind. I need a place to hide
for a few days. Somewhere no one can find us."

"Us?"

"I'll be bringing a woman and her daughter with me. They're on the run. They're in trouble, Daniel. I'm involving Annie."

His friend let out a slow sigh. "Bring them here. No one but CTC knows of our connection. Besides, Raven would love to see you."

Stefan strode across the camp where Faith and Zoe still struggled with the tent. "I'll owe you one."

"That's what friends are for, Stefan."

"Thanks, Daniel."

His friend hung up, and Stefan slipped his earpiece back into his pocket. They folded the tent and he loaded it, slamming the back end shut. "That took fifteen minutes. Come on, we're out of here."

Faith and Zoe jumped into his SUV and he joined them. "We have a place to lie low," he said, yanking the car into gear.

"We'll be safe?" Faith asked. "You're sure?"

Stefan sped across the desert, the sand kicking up behind him. "He won't find you. I promise."

THE TEXAS MORNING sun hadn't peeked over the tall buildings of downtown Dallas. Burke's Mercedes whizzed west, leaving the city behind, past too many exits to count. He headed through Fort Worth and finally came upon the Weatherford exit, but he couldn't return to the Shiny Penny. It was too soon.

He gripped the steering wheel until his knuckles whitened. Every nerve ending under his skin fired until he could hardly bear the stinging.

His father didn't understand. Burke wasn't some self-indulgent child. He had to feed his needs or he would explode.

He gripped the armrest just as his cell phone rang.

Burke tapped his Bluetooth receiver on the steering wheel. "Thomas."

"It's Orren. I found them."

At the news, Burke's heart raced. "You have Faith and Zoe?"

"I said I found them. And their cowboy friend. He shot down the drone and knew enough to take the hard drive and memory card before they bugged out. Their camp has been scrubbed clean. We caught a few fuzzy images during streaming, but there was a delay. We were too far away for clear reception."

Burke's knuckles whitened. "Who *is* this guy?"

"I got no leads. No one in this town talks to strangers." Orren cursed. "It's damned spooky. I couldn't even get the waitress at the diner to gossip."

Burke's neck and shoulders clenched. He gripped the steering wheel with a death-like force. "How will you find them?"

"Leave it to me. Your ex-wife doesn't have any family or friends, so my best bet is tracking this guy. I'm sending you several photos. We need your father's contacts to run them through enhancement and facial recognition software. Someplace that has military records. This guy is no cowboy."

"Done." Burke couldn't ask his father for a name,

of course, but he had access to his father's files. He'd find someone.

"By the way, boss. Your ex and the cowboy are *very* close, if you know what I mean. I have a photo of them in a lip-lock that practically melted the camera."

Burke's hands jerked. The car veered. He cursed before straightening out and pulling off the road.

He banged on the steering wheel, the fury rising up his neck. "I'll take care of the photos. You find Faith. I don't care how, just do it. Because if you don't, I'll find someone else who can. And you know what a canceled contract means."

Orren gulped through the phone. Burke relished the fear he could evoke with the simplest of words.

A woman in a convertible passed his Mercedes and pulled over. Her blond hair whipped in the wind as she backed up on the side road.

She turned to him and smiled. "Need some help?"

Burke grinned back. Just his type.

He glanced in the back seat. His kit was packed. The Smiley Face Killer had been his latest research project. He'd even included yellow chalk to mark her.

His father could go to hell.

"My phone died," he said. "May I use yours?"

She glanced at him and then his car, the smile in her eyes deepening. "I think I can trust a Mercedes man."

"You can." He pasted on the expression that had gained him trust from all of his victims. "My name is Burke."

"I'm Shanna."

"Well, Shanna. You have a beautiful smile."

NOON IN WEST Texas brought the sun beating down, especially in late summer. Faith leaned forward and turned up the air conditioner. They'd been traveling over dirt roads alternating with paved for hours, and she had no idea where they were headed. The West Texas landscape didn't hold a lot of distractions, much less unique landmarks. No matter which road he turned onto, nothing changed.

Faith sent Léon a sidelong glance. "You haven't told me exactly where we're headed." She didn't like getting the silent treatment.

"We're meeting my boss to switch vehicles in case the drone picked up the license plate." Stefan glanced at his watch. "After that, I'm taking you to a friend's house."

Faith couldn't stop the gulp that seemed to echo through the car. "My situation has already caused you to leave *your* home." She scooted across the seat closer to him and lowered her voice. "Zoe and I should disappear. Like we planned."

"He's got the scent now, Faith." His low voice rumbled in his chest. "I'll hide you until I can connect with Annie. In the meantime, I'd like to see if there's a way we can stop *him*—" he glanced over his shoulder at Zoe "—without you two being forced on the run for the rest of your lives."

"It can't be done," she whispered with a tone of resignation lacing her voice. "Just give me Annie's contact information. It's the only choice. We both know it."

"Give me the chance to fix this for you. I have the

resources. In the meantime, I can keep you two safe. I promised, didn't I?"

His voice rose a bit, and his challenging scowl caused Faith to sigh inside. Just what she needed. Another person even more stubborn than Zoe in her life.

"Léon always keeps his promises, Mom. He told me." Zoe munched on a bag of chips behind them.

Faith's head whipped around to stare at her daughter. How much had Zoe heard? Faith couldn't read her face. Zoe simply looked at Léon with complete adoration. She was his biggest fan.

"Good to know," Faith muttered. "I can't be in the dark like this. I need—"

"To control your life. I get that." Léon had the grace to wince. "Sorry. I'm used to working alone. We're closing in on the first rendezvous point to meet the head of CTC, Ransom Grainger. I'll give you Annie's number then."

They turned down another dirt road. Dust kicked up behind them, leaving a visible cloud ten feet in the air.

Two vehicles waited just ahead. Léon pulled up beside them, before reaching across her to snag a notebook out of the glove box. He scribbled a phone number. "Don't use this until I have a chance to call Annie," he warned. "She takes her privacy very seriously."

Faith pocketed the number and nodded.

"Wait here," he said, and exited the vehicle.

He crossed over to the two men. Faith rolled down the window. She wasn't about to be in the dark about her own situation.

"Ransom," Léon said, and shook a tall man's hand.

From what Faith could see, Ransom Grainger would intimidate most people. His black hair added to his intense demeanor, and his dark brown eyes were cold and calculating. His appearance alone made Faith shiver. She wouldn't want to be on the wrong side of that man.

She strained to hear what they were saying.

"What's their story?" Ransom asked Léon with a skeptical frown.

Léon's brow arched. "Why are you asking?"

"Because about an hour ago an image of you popped up in a federal-agency-wide facial recognition sweep."

Léon paled. Faith couldn't have imagined him ever appearing scared, but he did.

"What's wrong with Léon, Mom?" Zoe asked. "He looks like he's going to be sick."

"Shh, Zoe. Let me listen."

"Damn it. The drone." He rubbed his face. "Faith was right. Her ex-husband's family's got a lot of contacts." He looked at Ransom. "So, how bad is it?"

"Let's just say it's a good thing you've got Annie working on a new identity, even though there was no reason for you to leave Carder," Ransom said in a curt voice. "Now there's every reason. You've been made."

The statement hit Faith in her chest, forcing the air from her lungs. He was in trouble just like her. He had to disappear, too.

"Are you just assuming? Maybe—"

"The chatter's up, and I'd say in the next twenty-four to forty-eight hours, your enemies will be landing in Texas to vie for a $20 million price on your head. There's even a $1 million reward for proof you're alive."

Faith pressed her hand against her mouth. What had she done? She should never have agreed to let Léon help them. The Thomas family had put Léon's life in danger, but it was her fault.

"He's that desperate?" Léon asked. "Twenty million will buy just about anyone." He paced back and forth and looked over his shoulder right at her.

She made her expression go blank. He narrowed his gaze slightly, but she simply stared out the window, struggling not to show the anguish shredding her heart. She didn't want him to know she'd heard every word.

"Do Logan and Katherine know?" Léon asked with a frown.

Ransom nodded. "Your sister and brother-in-law are upset. They'd hoped to rendezvous with you on their next visit to the ranch. They know if you leave, they may never see you again."

"They're in danger now that my enemies know I'm alive. They'll go after anyone who cares about me for leverage. You know that."

"Luckily, your sister has the best security in place. Logan won't let anyone near her or the kids."

Léon crossed his arms, his expression more intense than Faith had ever seen.

"There's only one way to protect my family, Ransom. Someone needs to earn that million dollars and I have to die again. Publicly."

"I know."

Faith turned her head and looked at Zoe. Her little

brow had furrowed. "Is Léon in trouble, Mom? Can we help him?"

"I'm going to try, Slugger." Faith's mind whirled with possibilities. She had her money back. She stuffed her hand into her pocket and fingered the piece of paper he'd given her.

"You have a day to help me get Faith and Zoe into a safe house," Léon said. "Then I'll worry about me."

"Eighteen hours," Ransom countered. "I'll scrub your vehicle. The license plate number appeared in the chatter. You can take one of mine. It's clean."

Léon rubbed his chin. "Deal."

Ransom dropped a set of keys into Léon's hand and glanced over at the car, meeting Faith's gaze. She swallowed hard. His expression had turned thoughtful, contemplative. Faith shifted on the seat. What was it with these men in Carder that made her shiver? It's as if they could see right into her mind and soul.

"Running isn't the answer for her and the little girl," Ransom said, as if he were speaking to her, not Léon. "We can help. That's what CTC does."

Léon shook his head. "I offered several times. She doesn't trust that *anyone* can guarantee their safety. I have to honor her wishes, Ransom."

"At the expense of your life?"

Léon didn't answer. Faith leaned back in the front seat and closed her eyes. She'd been right to run in the first place. She'd been wrong to get him so involved, and she could only think of one way to fix the problem. It wouldn't be easy. But it might work.

If she was smart and quick.

"Let's transfer your belongings into my truck," Ransom said.

Faith twisted in her seat and lowered her voice. "Slugger, I need you to pretend you're asleep for a few minutes, okay?"

Her daughter's eyes grew confused. "Why?"

"We're playing a little trick on Léon, okay? Don't let him know you're awake."

She grinned. "Okay, Mom."

Faith hated lying to Zoe, but it was for Léon's own good.

He walked back to the vehicle. "We're taking the white truck. No one will be able to track us."

With everything inside of her, she struggled to remain calm. He was too intuitive not to guess her intentions. She couldn't let anything slip. "Good."

At her staccato response, he narrowed his gaze at her. "Are you okay?"

She let out a small yawn and blinked at him. "Just tired. Like Zoe." Faith nodded at the back seat.

"Asleep?"

"She couldn't stay awake any longer. It's been a tough couple of days."

"I'll carry her."

"No, I'll take her. Keys?"

Léon handed them to her. Faith opened up the back door and pulled Zoe into her arms.

Ransom tipped his hat to her. "Ma'am."

She didn't know what to say to him. She slipped Zoe into the vehicle and hurried back to the SUV. Her timing had to be just right. She grabbed her duffel and Zoe's orange knapsack.

Luck was with her. Léon, Ransom and another cowboy headed to the back of the SUV to unload the camping equipment.

With hands shaking, Faith scooted into the front seat and shut the door as quietly as she could. It closed with a soft snick.

She turned the engine on and without hesitation slammed it into gear and took off across the desert.

Léon stared after her, stunned, along with the two other men.

Within a few hundred yards she hit pavement. She never looked back.

Someday, she'd send money to pay for the truck, but for now, she had to protect Léon.

She'd head to Mexico and disappear. She refused to let anyone else get hurt because of her.

Chapter Eight

The sun hung low in the sky and shadows painted the desert. Stefan slammed his hand against the steering wheel. Faith and Zoe had vanished. He'd been a fool to try to help. He was still a fool to search for them.

Faith had left no trail to follow.

A very small part of him admired the hell out of her gumption. He kneaded the back of his neck. As a last resort he'd asked Zane, CTC's computer expert, to run a background check on Faith's ex-husband. Except for a few late child support payments, he'd come up squeaky clean. Too perfect, actually.

He squinted through the failing light. He was out of options and no closer to finding them.

His phone rang. After a quick glance at the screen, he tapped his earpiece. "Ransom?"

"Did you give her Annie's number?"

The curt question caused Léon to groan. "I instructed Faith not to call the number until I spoke with Annie personally."

"She's not too happy with you. Her number is a sacred trust. What were you thinking?"

"That Faith is hiding from a serial killer who found her in the middle of nowhere." Stefan winced despite his excuse. "I'm in deep trouble with Annie, aren't I?"

"I'd get used to permanent groveling. *If* she forgives you." Stefan recognized the frustration in Ransom's voice. "On the other hand, Annie normally would've left us in the dark. Instead, she called to let me know Faith and her daughter were at the trailer."

The world had just tilted on its access. "Annie never reveals her clients. Even if we're the go-between. Why?"

"She discovered a $250,000 reward on the dark web. Too many people are looking for them."

"Annie would've already moved her camper by now. Where are they?"

Ransom gave Stefan the GPS coordinates. He cut a sharp U-turn. Next stop: Annie's.

Two hours later, the sun had set and Stefan's headlights pierced the night. He drove over a small rise and when he hit the top, a lantern beamed at him from the distance.

Almost there.

What was he supposed to say to Faith when he saw her? She was an adult. She could make her own mistakes. Why in the hell was he driving in the middle of nowhere trying to find her when she clearly didn't want his help?

Because he was an idiot, and for some reason Faith and Zoe had inserted themselves into a soft, squishy place he'd believed he'd eradicated a long time ago.

He parked his truck next to the one Faith had stolen and exited the vehicle.

Annie stepped out of the trailer, hands on her hips. He winced at the expression on her face. He raised his hands. "I'm sorry, Annie. I just—"

"I know exactly what happened. One look at Faith and that kid of hers and you melted into a puddle of primordial ooze. Just so you know, I've changed my number, and you don't get it." She opened the door and shook her head in disgust. "Swallow your apology and come in. Zoe's going to be happy to see you. Faith, not so much."

"She stole Ransom's truck," he said with a bemused shake of his head.

Annie chuckled. "I'd have loved to have seen his face when she took off. And yours."

"We weren't expecting her to do something so damned crazy." Stefan scowled at her, but Annie simply smiled and led him inside.

At least she wasn't angry enough to shoot him.

He followed her into the camper.

Faith sat at the makeshift table with Zoe. When he strode in, she shot to her feet. "What's he doing here?" She whirled on Annie. "You called him! I thought I could trust you."

"Zoe," Stefan said with a wink. He held the latest and greatest handheld device up. "I brought you a game and some earphones."

Zoe's eyes got big. "Really? Danny had one at home, and I used to play—"

Stefan placed it in her hands and she shot a pleading glance to her mother. "Please?"

"Just for a while." Faith shot Stefan a withering glare while Zoe bundled down in the recliner with her new game. "Are you trying to buy her off? That's one of Burke's tricks."

"Maybe I didn't want her to hear that every criminal on both sides of the border is looking for you both to earn a nice finder's fee."

"How much?"

When he told her, she lost all color and sank into a dining chair. "What can we do?"

"What you should've done in the first place. Let me help you." He faced Annie. "How long to create a new identity for them?"

"I can turn the birth certificates and driver's license around in a day. It'll take longer to backstop her identity, though."

"I can work with that. We'll disappear for a few days." Stefan stared down Faith. "You're coming with me. No more running."

"Can't we stay with Annie?" She sent a pleading glance to the woman.

The plea shouldn't have hurt, but it cut Stefan to the core. Why couldn't she trust him?

"I'm sorry, honey," Annie said. "I've got clients whose lives depend on secrecy. It just wouldn't work." She glared at Stefan.

"What about a motel?" Faith chewed on her bottom lip and met Stefan's gaze. "I know people are coming for you. I heard your boss. Your life is in danger because of me. If you're not with us you can disappear."

"Faith—"

Annie let out a sharp curse.

"It was only a matter of time before my previous life caught up with me." Stefan forced an uncaring shrug. "Speaking of which, is my new passport ready?"

Annie shook her head. "You said you weren't in a hurry, but I can have it the same time as theirs."

Stefan crossed his arms and glared at Faith. "You blew my cover, darlin'. You owe me and I'm collecting. For now, we stay together, we get out of town and we hunker down. Agreed?"

"I think you're making a mistake." Faith sank into the bench behind the table. "I was only doing what I thought was the right thing. I was trying to protect you."

"That's my job. Not yours." He studied her, baffled. When had anyone ever cared enough to sacrifice for him? He knelt next to the table and took one of her hands. "Let me finish this, Faith. Let me keep you and Zoe out of Burke's hands."

She lifted her head and he met the tired gaze in her red-rimmed eyes "I should be able to handle my own problems. Burke was mine."

"We all need help sometimes," Annie said quietly. "Léon knows what he's doing."

Stefan squeezed her fingers. "You may have believed you were fighting this battle alone, but you're not anymore. Burke's my problem now, too."

THE WOMAN'S DEATH hadn't satisfied. Burke struggled to slip the key into the lock of his condominium. His hand trembled. Drawing that stupid smiley face near her body, mimicking the Smiley Face Killer, had been anticlimactic at best. He needed a more hands-on approach to the body. More up-close-and-personal time.

Burke pushed open the door of his home. The place was elegant, pristine and perfect. White, black, glass and metal. Without a stick of mahogany anywhere. Exactly how he wanted his life.

He set down his kit on the entryway table. The thrumming in his veins had dissipated, but it hadn't left him. The urge remained.

He now understood. He needed a more personal kill. He relished witnessing the life fade from their eyes, hearing them beg for mercy, but he needed more time with them. To touch them, to cut them, to make them his own.

The urge, the desire, grew stronger by the minute. He'd have to find someone else. Tonight.

"You broke your promise to me." His father's voice pierced the darkness. "Again."

Burke spun around.

His father flipped on the lamp in the living room. A tall glass of whiskey sat in front of him. He took a sip. "Why?" he asked. "Why can't you stop?"

The fatigue on his father's face surprised Burke. Weakness? His father never showed anything less than strength.

Gerard Thomas swirled the drink around. "Maybe

I should have told the authorities about Heather when you were sixteen. That was a mistake, I think. I thought you'd grow out of it. I thought you'd learn self-control."

Heather. When was the last time Burke had heard her name aloud? His one true love. His first. In everything. She'd just turned eighteen when she'd gone to work for his father. Burke had been doing time in the mailroom when he'd first seen her. Beautiful, pure blond hair, a waiflike figure who wore clothes like a New York model. Passionate lips and hands that had brought him more pleasure than he'd ever known. His ideal. His passion. His only love.

His father set the glass down with a clink. "I can't cover for you anymore, Burke. You need help I can't give you."

Burke straightened his back, shoving the past away. "I'm *fine.* I don't need your interference. I can see to my own affairs."

"You're not fine. You killed again. You've hired a man who can't be trusted to deal with your ex-wife. You've become reckless." He paused. "I've decided you need professional help."

"What have you done?" Burke stilled and knotted his fist.

"I found a place overseas. They'll be…discreet. They will teach you discipline, how to control your urges. When you're better, you can return."

"You're sending me away? To what? Some hospital?"

"It's a facility that deals with…difficult cases."

"You SOB." Needles of fury pricked the back of Burke's neck. "You're committing me, aren't you? You want me to disappear."

"Just until you're better."

The placating tone grated on Burke's already-raw nerves. He paced back and forth, shaking his head with force. The man would ruin all his plans. He needed to think. He had to clear his brain from the roar echoing in his skull. He faced his father. "I'll have Faith soon. I'll stop her. I'll get Zoe back for Mom. That's what you wanted, isn't it?"

"You're taking too many girls. They're being noticed." His father rose and grabbed Burke by the shoulders. "Look me in the eye and tell me you can stop."

"Of course I can."

"That's what you said after Heather."

"You don't get to talk to me about her. She threatened to tell Mom about your affair with her," Burke spat out. "What was I supposed to do?"

His father's head snapped around. "What?"

"She was mine!" Burke shouted. "You had to put your filthy hands on her, and she threatened to tell. I couldn't let her hurt Mom. I killed her *because of you*." Burke crossed the room until he loomed above his father. When had the man gotten so old? "You didn't call the cops because you *knew* Mom would find out. She'd divorce you and her family's money would drive you out of business."

His father's face slackened with shock.

"I didn't know then, but I'm in the company now.

I'm good at what I do, Father. I studied the history, believing you were something you're not."

Burke walked over to the bar and pulled a small leather pouch from a drawer. He'd been prepared for this day from the moment he'd divorced Faith. He poured himself a double and downed the whiskey in one gulp before unzipping the kit. A syringe and small vial lay protected inside.

Filling the syringe didn't take long. He returned to his father.

"You're taking drugs now?"

"This isn't for me," Burke said with a smile.

He grabbed his father's left hand. The whiskey fell to the floor. In one motion Burke jabbed the needle at the base of his ring finger and plunged all the way.

His father stared at his hand. "What have you done?"

"What I should have done years ago."

His father shot to his feet. Burke shoved him back to the sofa. He recognized the fear lacing his father's eyes. His chest swelled with satisfaction.

"I protected you." His father clutched his chest. "I've saved you countless times. You'll get caught without me."

"You taught me well." Burke pinned the man he'd hated for fifteen years to the sofa. "I'll never get caught."

FAITH COULDN'T STOP staring at the white center lane on the West Texas road. The blurring line mesmerized her. Or maybe it was the lack of sleep. She'd tossed and turned in the fold-out bed Annie had provided her and Zoe until about four this morning.

The dreams had come feverishly. Léon reaching out to her and someone jerking him away. The visions had all ended the same way, with them lying on the ground in a pool of blood, Burke standing over them laughing, Zoe at his side.

She'd called out at least once because in the early morning hours, Léon had lain down beside her, pulled her into his arms and held her close the rest of the night. He'd been nothing but a gentleman. She'd finally settled in and given in to sleep.

Three hours hadn't been enough to wash away the dreams, though. Her entire body felt as if she'd been chewed up and spit out by a harvester. Faith rubbed her tired eyes just as Stefan turned the truck down a long, winding driveway. He paused briefly in front of an iron gate. It swung open and the truck shuddered when they crossed a cattle guard.

They'd been on the road for at least four hours, but following his indirect route had been impossible. She had no idea where they were. She didn't want to ask.

A ranch-style house sat at the end of the paved road. There had to be at least five acres around it. Faith could even make out a barn behind the main house. The lawn surrounding the house appeared a bit odd, actually, in the midst of the desert plants.

Two girls, a year or two younger than Zoe, ran through a sprinkler system in the front yard. Every few seconds a huge reddish dog forced his face into the water before shaking all over and sending the girls into fits of laughter.

Léon pulled into the driveway. "We're here."

Faith glanced at him, worry weighing down her shoulders. "What if Burke—?"

"Do you think I'd do anything to place this family in danger?" he asked, his tone sharp.

She bit her lip. Faith should trust him. She did, actually, but Burke... She'd never known him to give up. He always won.

Could this time be different? With a sigh, she sent him a sidelong glance before finally nodding.

Zoe looked through the car's window with longing. "Can I play?" she asked, though from her tone she expected another *no*.

Léon turned in his seat. "You can play all you want here," he said. "We're staying for a day or two."

"Good. I'm tired of driving." Zoe grinned at him.

A tall man with a slight limp walked toward the truck. Léon rolled down the window and smiled. The first truly relaxed smile Faith could remember seeing on his face.

"Daniel. Good to see you, my friend."

The faint accent thickened with his greeting. Maybe because Léon had let his guard down?

"And who might you have with you?" Daniel asked, peering into the SUV, the scar down the side of his cheek taking nothing away from his compelling features.

"This is Faith, and the girl eager to jump into the fun is Zoe. Faith and Zoe, this is my friend Daniel

Adams." Léon flicked the unlock button on the console and opened his door. "You're free, Zoe."

Her daughter nearly bounced out of the back seat onto the ground and raced around the truck to stare at the front yard with longing.

Faith couldn't remember her daughter being so excited since the first day of baseball practice earlier this spring. A familiar wave of guilt settled in her gut. She'd wanted so much more for Zoe than being on the run the rest of their lives.

Faith exited the vehicle and rounded the truck. She placed her left hand on Zoe's shoulder and reached out her right to Daniel. "Thank you for taking us in."

He smiled at her. "Any friend of Léon's." Daniel turned to the yard and cupped his hands around his mouth. "Christina. Hope. Come here, girls."

They veered from their play and the dog followed. He bounded toward Faith and Zoe.

"Trouble. Sit," Daniel ordered.

Before the dog could jump on them, he dropped his rump. His tail wagged and the huge animal had what appeared to be a smile on his face. His entire body vibrated with excitement.

"He won't bite. He's just excitable. And yes, he was named after the town." Daniel smiled down at the two girls. "These are my daughters, Christina and Hope."

"It's so nice to meet you," Faith said. "This is Zoe."

Her daughter took a few steps until she was toe-to-toe with the little girls. "You look alike."

Hope grinned. "We're twins. We're five. Do you want to play?"

Zoe glanced over her shoulder at Faith.

"Sure. Just stay close."

Zoe grinned wide.

"Come on, Trouble," Hope called.

A woman joined Daniel and she gave Léon a hug. "It's good to see you."

"This is my wife, Raven," Daniel said.

Raven gave Faith a welcoming albeit sympathetic smile. "From what I gathered you've had a tough few days. How about some sun tea?"

She hesitated, glancing at Zoe.

Léon gave her a small nod. "Daniel has a surveillance system. If anyone opens the gates without permission, he'll know it. Zoe is safe here."

Raven squeezed Faith's arm. "Daniel and Léon will watch over them. Come on inside."

Zoe ran through the sprinkler, laughing and shaking her head. Water sprayed from her. How long had it been since she'd heard that kind of carefree laugh from her daughter?

Until Léon came into their lives?

Faith followed Raven into the house, through the welcoming living room and into the kitchen. She poured tea over ice. Faith sat at the large rectangular oak table and took a long sip.

She could breathe in this house. No one could tie her to Daniel and Raven Adams. And who would come looking for them in a house outside of a town she'd never heard of? She hadn't known Trouble, Texas, existed.

"Delicious," she said with a sigh.

"You can't beat sun tea," Raven said, wiping down the counter. "Barbecue okay for a late lunch? That way Daniel does most of the cooking." Raven grinned. She placed a stockpot of water on the stove and dumped a bag of potatoes into the sink.

"Can I help?" Faith asked.

Raven scooted over and handed her a potato peeler. "I never refuse an extra pair of hands."

The women worked silently for a while. Raven placed a clean potato off to the side. "If you're wondering, Léon didn't tell us what you're going through, just that you're in trouble." She picked up another vegetable and slid the peeler along the skin. "Daniel and I met because he saved my life. He and Trouble found me buried alive. You can trust my husband and Léon to protect you and your daughter. I have the experience to prove it."

Faith gaped at Raven.

"Long story, but we found my daughters and have a good life. We're even adopting a little boy next month." Raven placed her hand on Faith's. "My point is life can get better. You've found a good man willing to do whatever it takes to help you, and that man has some friends who've gotten people out of more trouble than you can imagine."

Faith had rarely seen the kind of confidence Raven displayed in anyone, much less experienced it. She'd come with Léon because she couldn't figure out another way to protect Zoe. Inside, that wall she'd built around her heart had weakened a bit. Her response to him terrified her.

Burke's betrayal had practically destroyed her. She'd vowed not to rely on anyone else. She couldn't afford to give away her power like that.

Faith's head hurt from all the scenarios she worked through in her mind. She and Raven continued in silence until the three girls rushed into the kitchen.

"Mom, when are we eating?" Zoe asked.

"Not for a while yet."

The twins groaned. "We're hungry," they said in unison.

Raven nodded toward a bowl of sliced fruit and cheese. "I know my daughters well. Sit at the table to eat."

Three chairs scraped the floor. The girls giggled and scarfed down their snack. Soon they were whispering quietly.

"What do you think that's about?" Faith asked Raven in a low voice.

Raven frowned. "Trouble, if I know my girls."

ZOE SAT AT the table, eyeing her mom before examining the last nectarine slice. Today had been the best day in a long time. She'd gotten so tired of being cooped up in the library all the time. Especially when her mom made her practice her reading all day long.

"You take it," Hope said with a smile, pushing the plate to her.

Zoe didn't usually play with girls, especially not little girls who were only five, but Hope and Christina weren't like other girls. Plus, it was so cool that they looked exactly alike.

With a smile, Zoe popped the nectarine slice into her mouth.

Hope shoved back her chair. "Come on," she said. "Let's go to our room. We can play there."

Zoe stood up, but paused for a moment. "Do you ever talk?" she asked Christina.

The girl nodded.

"Not really," Hope interrupted. "She doesn't like to."

Zoe followed the girls to a large room. Twin bunk beds lined up against one wall opposite huge shelves with tons of toys. Zoe wrinkled her nose. Mostly dolls and girl stuff on the left side, but on the right side, a bunch of board games were stacked up, along with a soccer ball.

A soft scratch sounded at the door.

"Trouble!" Christina shouted.

The dog trotted in and plopped in the center of the floor.

Christina climbed onto his back and hugged him. "My daddy said you don't have a place to live."

Zoe's eyes widened. "I thought you didn't talk."

Hope grinned. "She talks, just not much. And mostly when Trouble's nearby."

Christina stroked his fur. "Do you miss your house?" She stared at Zoe from astride the huge dog.

A small pang in the center of her chest made Zoe sad for a moment. "I miss playing baseball with my friend, Danny. And I miss my daddy. He promised to take me to a baseball game this summer, and summer's almost over. Plus, he buys me neat toys. He got me a tablet a while back and it wasn't even my birthday."

The twins' mouths dropped open. "Wow. Where is it?"

"My mom made me leave it when we ran away. She and my dad don't like each other." Zoe sat in front of Trouble and patted his head. "You're lucky you have a dog. I wish I had one. My mom said I could get a puppy, but then we left home. I don't know if I'll *ever* have one now." She let out a long, drawn-out sigh.

Hope grinned and stared at her sister.

Christina nodded at her twin. "Wanna see something?"

From the expressions on the twins' faces, Zoe knew whatever they were going to look at had to be good. She followed her new friends out the back door, across the lawn and into a big barn. Christina put her finger over her lips. "Shh. We have to be quiet. We might wake them up."

They shut the door behind them and opened up a gate just inside the building. A bunch of squeaks erupted and a half-dozen balls of fur zoomed at them.

A dog that looked kind of like Trouble lay in the corner and sort of smiled at them.

"Puppies," Zoe said, her eyes wide. "You have puppies."

"Come on. Sit down."

Hope and Christina plopped down on the hay in the center of the pen, and Zoe joined them. The puppies scrambled all over them.

Zoe giggled. The smallest puppy pushed its nose into her side. She picked up the reddish brown furball with big eyes and white splashes around her eyes and mouth. In less than a minute, Zoe fell in love.

She held the puppy in her arms and the little animal buried itself in her shoulder.

"Mom said we have to give them all away to good homes," Christina said with a frown. "So other little girls and boys can play with them."

"Do you want one?" Hope asked.

Zoe jumped to her feet and hugged the little furball tight. "I want this one. She likes me."

"Zoe!" her mother's voice sounded panicked.

She ran out of the barn and skidded up to her mother. Her mom was scared, and Zoe felt bad. Her mom didn't smile anymore, either. Except when Léon was around.

The puppy would cheer her mom up.

"Look." She cradled the little dog in her arms and walked over to her mother. "Hope and Christina said I could have her. I'm going to name her Catcher, 'cause she kinda looks like she has a face mask on."

Her mother knelt down and Zoe got that twist back in the pit of her stomach. She recognized the look on her mom's face.

"Zoe. We're moving around a lot. A puppy needs a backyard to play in."

It wasn't fair. They used to have a backyard. Her grandma and grandpa had a huge yard. Her daddy had a yard, even though Zoe had never seen him go outside at his house.

"You're just saying that. We could go home and have a place for Catcher. You took away my house and my friends and my daddy. I hate you."

Zoe shoved Catcher at Christina and ran into the house. She'd had enough of this so-called vacation her mom had taken her on. She wanted to go home.

Chapter Nine

The barn went awkwardly silent. The screen door slammed against the jamb, and Zoe's footsteps pounded away. Faith took in a shuddering sigh and pinched the bridge of her nose.

Raven placed her arm on Faith's shoulder and gave her a sympathetic smile. "She's probably gone upstairs to the girls' room. If I'm right, here comes the door."

Sure enough, a second door slammed closed.

Faith closed her eyes. "I'm so sorry."

"I may not know much about what you're going through," Raven said, "but it's obvious Zoe's been through a lot."

"Thank you for being so kind." Faith wanted to sink into the floor despite Raven's understanding. "I need to talk to her."

Faith left Raven and her daughters and headed inside the house. She trudged up the stairs. She hated this. Why couldn't she have said *yes*? She wanted to give in. Zoe had lost so much, and was about to lose more even though she didn't realize it yet. Faith's head throbbed from the base of her skull all the way to her temples.

Maybe she'd ask Raven and Daniel if they could take one of the puppies once she and Zoe settled.

Except, that wouldn't work. With new identities they wouldn't be able to contact anyone from their past life. Annie had been very clear about the rules…and the consequences. She and Zoe were stuck, painted into a corner by Burke—and her own choices.

Faith hadn't felt so insecure as a mother since the first day she'd brought Zoe home from the hospital. Or maybe the day she'd left Burke's mansion and taken Zoe to the rental house Faith couldn't really afford.

She reached the top of the stairs. Of the five doors she could see, only two were closed. Faith knocked on the first one and cracked it open. She peered into the guest room, searched the closet, the bathroom and even under the bed. Zoe wasn't anywhere to be found.

One room down, one to go. She rapped on the door. No answer. She knocked again. "Zoe, I know you're in there. Come on, let's talk about it."

Her daughter didn't respond.

She inched open the bedroom door and stepped into the twins' room. Faith wanted her daughter to have a room like this one, except maybe she'd have sports equipment and Erector Sets instead of dolls and board games.

Faith crouched down and glanced under the bed. Zoe wasn't here, either. She rose, scanned the room and her gaze honed in on the closet. Perfect hiding place. Zoe had been known to disappear in small spaces from the time she was a toddler.

Faith pressed it open. Zoe sat on the floor, her back facing her mother. With a long inward sigh, Faith sat cross-legged next to Zoe.

"I'm sorry, but we can't go home, Slugger. And we can't bring the puppy with us. Not until we have a place to live. I promise, when I find us a house—"

"I didn't want a dog anyway," Zoe said, her voice catching with emotion. "They're too much trouble."

She tugged some blocks from the corner of the closet. "I'm busy right now. I want to be alone."

Zoe swiped at her face.

Faith placed her hands on Zoe's shoulders. "Honey—"

"Can I be alone, Mom? I don't want to talk right now."

The words were so quiet, so disheartened, but Faith knew her daughter well. Sometimes she needed space. Kind of like her mother. Faith rose to her feet. "I *am* sorry, Zoe. Soon, everything will be better."

"Sure."

Her daughter ducked her head. The flat tone hurt Faith's heart, but it couldn't be helped. She had no other choice. With one last backward glance, she exited the room and headed downstairs. She met the twins racing up. They stopped and looked at her.

"Is Zoe okay?" Hope asked.

Faith forced a smile. "She'll be fine. Maybe you'd like to play with her? I think she could use a couple of friends."

The girls ran to their room and burst inside before closing the door behind them. Faith hovered outside for a moment, but she couldn't make out what the girls were saying.

"Tough love?" Léon asked from the top of the staircase.

"The toughest." Faith met his sympathetic gaze. She rubbed the bridge of her nose. "I hate this. I want to let her have that puppy more than anything. She's been a trouper since all this started."

A dose of giggling sounded through the door, and Faith recognized Zoe's voice if not what she said. "At least she's talking to the twins."

Léon held out his hand. "Come with me. Hope and Christina are just what she needs right now. Maybe her mom needs a break, too?"

Faith gnawed at her lip, but after one last glance at the door, she followed him. He led her to the guest room and closed the door behind them.

Léon opened his arms, and she walked into them. Her body sagged, leaning against him. She shouldn't do it. She couldn't depend on him to comfort her, but she'd been alone for too long. Really since Zoe was born. She needed so badly to be held.

He stroked her hair.

"Going on the run isn't fair to Zoe," Faith whispered. "Nothing that's happened is her fault and she's paying the biggest price. How do I explain it?"

"She's a tough kid. She'll survive not having a puppy. She'll even survive this move. Kids are resilient. My nephew was kidnapped when he was little. He came through. So will Zoe."

Faith shook her head against his T-shirt. "I don't

know. She's lost everything in the last few months. What if she's not okay? What if I'm ruining her life?"

"You're doing what you have to do to protect her." He cupped her face; his blue eyes captured her gaze. "She loves you. She trusts you. You won't let her down."

"You really believe that?" Faith swiped at her eyes.

"She's got an amazing mother and role model. That's what I know."

"Thanks." She wanted to look away, but standing there, so close to him, she didn't want to move. She placed her hands on his arms. Her body leaned toward him.

"Léon—"

The blue of his eyes transformed to dark cobalt as he stared at her. He cupped her cheek and stroked down her skin. She leaned into his touch and took in a deep breath.

Ever so slowly, he lowered his mouth. She parted her lips and pressed against him. She wanted him to kiss her. Once more.

"Dinner," Raven called from down the stairs.

Léon stilled, his lips hovering just above hers. "Saved by the gong."

The deep, husky tone of his voice made her shiver. He didn't pull away. His hands drifted down her shoulders, past her elbows, until he threaded his fingers through hers.

She couldn't let this moment pass. She rose up and kissed him. The moment their lips touched, Léon groaned and folded her into his arms, pressing him hard against her, breast to chest, hip to hip.

He overwhelmed her with his mouth, claiming hers.

Her knees shook, and she clung to him, pulling him even closer.

"Hope, Christina. Now," Raven called out in that I'm-serious mom tone Faith used all too often.

With a reluctant moan, Léon lifted his lips. Faith couldn't mistake the hunger in his eyes, the want, the need. Her heart raced; her body tingled from her lips down deep into her belly.

He pushed her hair back from her temple. "I guess that means us, too."

Faith simply nodded.

A long sigh escaped him. "I shouldn't have. You know that."

"Maybe." She closed her eyes briefly. "But I'm not sorry, Léon."

He pressed his lips firmly against hers one last time. "Neither am I."

BURKE PACED BACK and forth. His father sat on the sofa, head lolled to the side. The man's breathing was shallow. His lips had turned blue and he'd grabbed his chest.

He was still breathing.

The bastard shouldn't have survived this long. And there he sat, in Burke's living room, still alive.

Damn it.

Burke itched to slice his throat. His hand reached behind him to the knife sheath. He could imagine each action. He relished the feel of the blade slicing through skin, the warm blood bathing his hands.

The light of life leaving the eyes.

It soothed him, drove away the needles of anxiety that prickled his skin.

Unfortunately, he couldn't use his father to provide the release he longed for. The world must believe Gerard Thomas had died of a heart attack.

That meant hands off.

Burke rubbed his temple. From everything he'd read at the medical school library, the potassium chloride should've worked. Really, it was the perfect poison. When they tested the old man's blood, the drug's metabolites would appear elevated, but the medical examiner would simply blame the levels on the muscle damaged caused by the heart attack.

What had gone wrong?

Had Burke made a mistake on the dosage? He picked up his phone, then paused. No, he couldn't search the internet. He'd watched enough cop shows to know they might review his browsing history.

He smiled. Maybe he could use his father's phone.

At that moment, his father convulsed on the sofa, his body twitching and jerking. He groaned once before going limp. His bowels emptied all over Burke's sofa.

The odor erupted through the house. Burke gagged. His father was still, but was he dead?

Burke stared at the grotesque image of his father lying in his own filth. The stain would never come out. He'd have to get a new sofa.

After rounding the couch, he reached out to feel for a pulse.

Nothing.

A flurry of triumph shot through his veins. Job done. He should have done this a long time ago.

The phone in his pocket vibrated. Hopefully Orren with good news.

He glanced down at the screen. Blocked call. He scowled. Perhaps the man had switched phones.

"Thomas."

"D-daddy?" Zoe's voice filtered through the earpiece.

Burke shook his head to clear his mind. "Zoe! Thank goodness you called. I've missed you so much, honey. Are you having fun on your vacation?"

"No. I miss you, Dad. Did you go to the baseball game like we planned?"

Burke cursed. He'd forgotten all about that stupid promise. "I couldn't go without you, Zoe. It wouldn't have been any fun. We all miss you and want you to come home. Your grandpa and grandma miss you, too. Where are you?"

She let out a sob. "I don't know. Outside a little town somewhere. We don't have a house anymore, Dad. We're staying with other people. They have puppies, and I want one, but Mom said no because we don't have a backyard."

"I have plenty of room for a puppy, Zoe." Burke gripped the phone tightly. "If you come home."

"I could bring Catcher with me? He's so cute and soft and—"

"You can have the puppy, Zoe, but I need to come get you if you're going to bring him home."

Zoe paused for a moment. "Mom wants me to live with her."

His daughter's voice had gone quiet and hesitant. Burke had to play this carefully.

"Your mom and I disagree, Zoe. But that's okay." He let out a long, slow breath and considered his next lie. "I love you enough to let you have a puppy. Maybe your mother doesn't."

A small sob and snotty sniffle escaped from Zoe. Kids really were disgusting.

"I don't know, Daddy. Mom would be all alone."

Some high-pitched whispers filtered through the phone. "We know our address," a little girl whispered.

Burke could've cheered. "Zoe? Please come home. Your mom can visit if she wants to." Of course, that would never happen.

His daughter had given him a gift. Once he knew Zoe's location, he'd know Faith's.

"I can bring Catcher?"

"Absolutely." Burke paused. "Where are you, Zoe?" He glanced over at his father's body. Everything was going to be fine.

THE KITCHEN BASKED in the scents of Southern barbecue and banana pudding. Stefan set down his spoon. "I don't know what you put in that ambrosia, Raven, but I could die happy now."

"Hey, what about me?" Daniel groused. "I grilled the chicken."

"She's domesticated you, that's for sure." Stefan leaned back in his chair and patted his belly. "If I hung out with you for a month, I'd weigh three hundred pounds."

The twins leaned toward each other and whispered. Stefan may not have children, but he recognized a plan being hatched. He leaned toward Christina. "What are you up to, little lady?"

Her eyes grew wide and frightened. "How did you know?"

Hope shushed her sister and Stefan forced himself not to grin. If only the bad guys he chased were as transparent as Daniel's twins. And Zoe.

Christina squirmed in her chair before turning toward her mother. "Can we be excused? Pleeease."

The plea went first to Raven, then Daniel.

"One more bite of green beans each," their father ordered.

They didn't even argue. Christina and Hope shoved a forkful of the vegetable in their mouths and stood up. They stared at Zoe.

Faith looked over at her daughter's nearly untouched plate. "Not hungry, Slugger?"

She shook her head, avoiding Faith's gaze.

"Okay," Faith said with a sigh. "I'm not going to force you."

Zoe shot to her feet. All three girls raced to the back door.

So that was their plan? Return to the barn? He wasn't sure it was a good idea for Zoe to get even more attached to the puppy. A little girl's heart was fragile, and Stefan didn't want it broken.

A bit shell-shocked at how the idea of her being hurt

pained him, he stilled. He'd never allowed himself to connect as quickly as he had with Zoe and Faith. No doubt his own heart would be battered and bruised by the time they parted ways.

The girls opened the back door, ready to escape the house.

"No more visits to the barn," Raven said, as if reading his mind. "Go upstairs and play."

Christina's face fell. "M…o…m."

"The puppies need their sleep and so does their mama." She glanced at her watch. "You have thirty minutes to play before bath time. I'd take advantage of it before I change my mind. Or you can always sit and listen to the grown-ups talk about the state of the economy and politics."

The three girls didn't hesitate. They closed the door and raced up the stairs.

"So, our conversation would bore them that much." Daniel chuckled.

Faith's gaze followed the girls' path. "I'm sorry Zoe's so moody. I just can't give her what she wants."

Daniel and Raven chuckled in sympathy. "Multiply it by two, and welcome to our world. She'll be okay."

Faith bit her lip. "I hope so."

"How about we take this into the library?" Daniel stood up. "Anyone want a drink?"

"Are you breaking out the good bourbon?" Stefan asked, escorting Faith and Raven through a set of French doors.

"While you're here, I can't go with the cheap stuff," his friend parried, sidling up to the bar.

"Then I'll sample a glass." Stefan touched the small of Faith's back. When she didn't pull away, he left his hand there, awareness rising within him.

"None for me," she said to Daniel's offer. "Sleep deprivation and alcohol don't mix."

Raven sat on one corner of a loveseat and tucked her feet underneath her, frowning in sympathy. "Do you know where you're headed?"

"Even if I did, I couldn't tell you. For everyone's safety." Faith glanced over at Stefan. "We'll disappear, and somehow, after we're gone, I have to explain to Zoe what her father is. I have no idea how to do that."

Stefan squeezed Faith's knee in comfort. "You're a psychologist, Daniel. Maybe you can help."

Faith gave Stefan a small nod and Stefan shared the basics of her dilemma. "Any suggestions?" he asked Daniel.

His friend let out a long whistle. "It's tough. I'm dealing with mostly veteran PTSD patients while I finish up my dissertation, so my expertise isn't child psychology, but I'd suggest being as honest as you can about what's happened. She must know your ex-husband had issues."

"If I didn't see it the entire time I was married to him—" Faith stared down at her nails "—how can I ask a seven-year-old to accept that the man she loves and trusts most in the world is a man who has murdered so many people?"

Daniel leaned forward in his chair. "The problem is, running away doesn't make sense to her. If you're going to make a success of your new life, your decisions need to be understandable to her, especially since protecting each other is the way your life will be. At least until he's caught."

Stefan slipped his hand into hers and squeezed. "There *are* other options."

He met Daniel's gaze, and his friend nodded.

"CTC can help," Daniel said. "Ransom Grainger, the head of CTC, has powerful connections. He'll use them if it means justice wins out."

Faith squirmed on the sofa. She tugged her hand from Stefan's grasp and crossed her arms. "So Stefan said, but I can't wait. Not with Burke so close to finding us. Not with the law on his side. If it goes wrong, he could take Zoe from me. I'm sorry. I can't risk it."

She glanced toward the stairs leading to the twins' bedroom and rose. "I've got to check on Zoe, then I'm going to bed." She turned to Raven and Daniel. "Thank you for putting us up. We appreciate it."

Raven stood and gave her a quick hug. "Trust them," she whispered. "They can help you."

Faith met Stefan's gaze and left the room.

He watched her leave and sipped on his bourbon. "I don't think she appreciated my PDA."

Daniel slapped him on the back of the head. "What were you thinking? As far as she's concerned, she'll never see you again once she leaves. Unless you two have agreed to be friends with benefits."

"Not Faith's style."

"Exactly," Daniel said.

"And that's my cue to exit and give the girls their bath." Raven stood and kissed Stefan on the cheek.

"You've changed since the last time you visited. Faith and Zoe are good for you. Don't let the baggage stand in your way. You two could have something."

She kissed Daniel a little too long for comfort. Stefan cleared his throat as she sashayed out of the room.

"I'd say the passion's still there."

"You could say that." Daniel cleared his throat. "Raven doesn't understand the risks staying together would bring to Faith. There've been too many CTC weddings in the last half-dozen years. My wife wants everyone to be happy."

"That's because you married an amazing woman. And one who's far too insightful."

"Truer words, but our path wasn't easy. You know that as well as anyone." Daniel closed the doors behind Raven. "What's going on with you, Stefan? You're involved. More than I've ever seen you."

Stefan paced the floor. "I don't know what I'm doing. Zoe… That little girl is fearless. She doesn't hold back. Faith…" He set his empty glass on the end table. "She's smart, she's beautiful and she's real, even while she attempts to keep everyone at arm's length. I look at her and I see her heart. How many people can you say that about?"

"Very few."

"I want what I can't have." Stefan paused at the end of the room and faced his friend. "Her ex destroyed her trust in others and herself. She knows she can't trust me—"

"You're wrong about that. She's put her life in your

hands by coming here. She trusts us by extension. She's let her guard down for you, Stefan."

He shoved his hand through his hair. "What am I supposed to do with that?"

Stefan stared at Daniel, more uncertain than he'd been since they were in that dungeon in Bellevaux, facing certain death.

"I make a round of the grounds every night, just to be safe."

"Paranoid much?" Stefan said.

"When it comes to my family," Daniel said, "absolutely."

They walked in silence for a while. The summer night's heat weighed upon Stefan, clinging like the past. The stark darkness made the world seem infinite.

Once they'd walked the perimeter they re-entered the house. "I can't tell you what to do, but I will remind you she took a leap of faith for you. You may want to do the same." Daniel strode over to Stefan and squeezed his shoulder. "Loving someone is the most terrifying risk I've ever taken."

More exasperated than ever, Stefan headed up the stairs. Raven and Faith met him outside the girls' bedroom.

"They asleep?" Stefan's body pulsed with frustration at how much remained out of his control.

A small fit of giggles filtered through the door.

"Pretending." Raven smiled.

"Though Zoe is still sulking," Faith said with a frown. "I'll give her until the morning, but she's got to accept my decision."

Stefan turned to Faith. "Can we talk?" Of course, he had no idea exactly what he was going to say to her.

Daniel joined them at the top of the stairs. "The house is locked up."

"Then we'll see you tomorrow morning." Raven held out her hand to Daniel, and he followed her into their bedroom.

Faith faced Stefan. He could see the indecision in her eyes.

"You don't have to be nervous," he said.

"How do you know what I'm feeling? It's kind of annoying."

"Because I'm feeling the same hesitation." He touched her cheek. "The truth is I'm tired of thinking."

"Me, too."

She pressed into his touch and her action made his heart swell. He led her into the guest room. "Let's sit."

Stefan pulled her to the edge of the bed and sat beside her, his knee touching hers. He twisted to face her. "I want to be with you, Faith. More than anything I've wanted in my life."

Her cheeks flushed. "I…I want you, too, but it's complicated."

"Another time, another place. It would still have been complicated." He cupped her cheek. His thumb grazed her silken cheek. He lost himself in her eyes. Those trusting eyes. "God, you look at me, and I forget everything. My past, my future. Your future."

"Maybe that's okay. We could forget everything. Just for tonight." She leaned into him. "Touch me before I change my mind, Léon."

The moment she uttered his alias, Stefan's entire body stilled. He met her passion-filled gaze and took in a deep breath.

"Not Léon. My real name is Stefan, Prince of Bellevaux."

Chapter Ten

A prince?

A loud gulp echoed in the guest bedroom over the cacophony of crickets outside. For a brief, horrifying moment, Faith realized it came from her.

"This is a joke, right?"

Stefan shifted, more uncomfortable than she'd ever seen him.

"Unfortunately, no. My real name is Stefan, Prince of Bellevaux."

Her mind whirled in confusion. "But…I remember the news story. There was a revolution. The two heirs to the throne were murdered. A woman from Texas became queen."

"My half sister, Kat." He cleared his throat. "I didn't know about her until after I was captured. She's Queen Katherine now."

Faith rubbed her temple. "You're a prince. Hiding out as some kind of spy?"

This couldn't be real.

"Why did you become Léon in the first place?" Her mind tried to understand, but she kept running into the obvious. "I know why I'm doing it. Because Burke is too powerful to fight. But why would a prince want to disappear? You have money and power."

"Not as much as you'd think." He removed his hand from hers and scratched his brow. "I never thought I'd be king. I was the stereotypical playboy second son until I completed graduate school in the States."

"I remember seeing your picture in the checkout line at the grocery store." She refused to tell him she'd always taken a second look at him. A real-life Prince Charming.

"I sold a lot of newspapers in those days." A chuckle escaped from him. "Everything was simple before I went home and served my two years in the military, like every other young man in my country. During my training they discovered I had a gift for long-distance shooting. I got pegged for a mission to verify rumors of a terrorist attack and stop it if we could."

"You succeeded." She didn't have to guess.

He shrugged. "I discovered I was good at black ops. My father was furious, but I'd found my calling. Until I killed the son of one of the terrorist leaders."

She gasped.

"A price went out on my head. Soon after the coup in Bellevaux took place, and the revolutionaries dumped me into the prison, sending out press releases I had been killed. They were planning to sell me to help fund their takeover of my country. Daniel and his team rescued me, but I was almost dead, and the hit was still in place. Even more so when the coup failed. They couldn't keep me safe."

He stood and paced the floor. "I had no choice. The people trying to kill me were in the shadows, they had operatives everywhere. Anyone near me would be at risk." He frowned at her. "Something for you to remember. If someone wants you dead badly enough, eventually they'll succeed. No matter what the security. You always have to be on your guard."

Faith shuddered at his flat statement because she knew he was right. But sometimes running was the only option.

Stefan stared out the bedroom window. "The palace didn't contradict the information that I'd been killed along with my brother. Kat became queen. I went into hiding."

She walked over to him, forcing him to face her. She studied his face. "You don't resemble the prince I remember from those papers or television."

He touched a small scar on his cheek that she'd barely noticed before now. "During my captivity, they broke a few bones. The shape of my face changed a little and I wear my hair longer and darker. I don't look completely different, but enough. Even if I tried to go back, I'm not sure the public would accept me. I not only look different, I am different. I can't be what they'd accept."

Faith took his hands in hers. "I'm so sorry. Because of the Thomas family, you have to start over again. After you've made friends and connections in Carder with CTC."

He lifted her fingers to his lips. "This is not your fault. Léon Royce has become someone I don't even like anymore. A black ops, sharpshooting expert who makes too many mistakes." He drew his knuckle down her face. "I would give anything to be normal again."

"Léon…" She shook her head. That wasn't his name. "Stefan." She chewed on the moniker. "It's not going to be easy calling you that. Léon saved Zoe's life. He's who I thought maybe…" Her voice trailed off.

What was she supposed to say? That somewhere in her mind, before she'd realized she'd put him in danger, before she'd realized who he was, she'd wondered if Léon would go with them? That she'd have a partner on this crazy journey she was about to embark on? She'd been more a fool than she'd thought. She'd done the worst thing she could possibly do. She'd come to rely on him.

"Do you prefer Léon?" he asked in a too-calm voice.

At his odd tone, she raised her gaze to his. Tension lined his eyes. His normal self-confidence had vanished. Discomfort and hesitation remained. For someone who'd lived under a false identity for years, he seemed oddly concerned by her response. "Léon's the man I grew to trust."

"Does my name matter that much to you?"

She chewed on the question for a moment. What was he really asking? "No matter what my name, I'm still me, right?"

He sat silent for a moment, not answering until she squirmed.

Her throat thickened. "Is Léon different from Stefan?"

Stefan considered her for a moment. "Do you want the truth?"

She nodded, now afraid of the answer.

"Changing your name changes you. Your new identity will change you. No matter how much you fight it, or how much you wish it didn't."

"Is it your life that changed you," she asked, "or your name?"

"Touché. It's hard to know after years of being Léon. Stefan is dead in so many ways. He died in that dungeon."

In a flash of insight she understood. They both felt trapped. "If you could do anything, go anywhere, what would you want your life to be like?"

She'd been afraid to ask herself that question.

"I'd want to have a chance to be with you," he said in a husky voice. "I'd want you and Zoe to come away with me, to be free from fear, free from looking over your shoulder."

He slipped his arms around her, and she rested her head against his shoulder as if she'd always meant to be there. With gentle hands, he stroked her hair and she didn't move. He felt strong and warm and solid. She never wanted to leave his embrace.

The cadence of night sounds filtered through the window. A soft breeze, the hoot of an owl, the buzz of cicadas.

"Why can't this last forever?" she whispered.

"Being in hiding doesn't give us the freedom to follow our hearts," he said softly. "Being smart will keep us safe."

"Am I a coward?" she asked. "For running."

"Power can be destructive. It can twist justice into

something perverted, but power used for good can level the playing field. I've always believed that."

From the tenor of his voice, she got the message. "You're talking about your friends," she said. "CTC couldn't help you?"

"It's different. Burke is one man."

Before she could respond Stefan's phone rang. "Speaking of which..." He tapped the screen. "What's up, Ransom?" Stefan frowned. "She's right here. I'll put you on speakerphone."

Faith leaned closer to the phone.

"Faith, I've been looking into your ex-husband to see if we can help you in your situation."

"I...I know. Stefan told me."

"Stefan. I see." Ransom paused for a moment. "I have some bad news."

Faith's heart stuttered. "What's wrong?"

"Gerard Thomas is dead. It appears to be a heart attack."

Her body went numb. "I...I don't understand. He was so healthy."

"You were close?" Ransom asked.

Faith shook in Stefan's arms. "Not really. He never wanted me to marry Burke. I think his wife, Janice... oh my gosh, she must be devastated. He and Burke are her entire world."

Ransom cleared his throat. "I need to ask you an awkward question. Would you say Gerard protected Burke? Maybe intervened over the years on his behalf?"

Grabbing the phone, Faith stepped away from Stefan. "What do you mean?"

"Your ex-husband's life is too…perfect."

"I…I don't understand."

"No one gets to be thirty without having some transgression on their record. A parking ticket, a few unpaid bills, a few photos that are less than flattering, but Burke's records are too clean. Which, frankly, has us wondering about some bought and sold influence."

"Mr. Thomas had friends across the state. People owed him favors. Burke threw the family name around a lot to get what he wanted. There was even talk of a run for governor."

Stefan joined her, and she hadn't realized how much she'd come to rely on his presence. His warm body pressed close to hers and he clasped the phone. "Ransom, if Gerard Thomas was willing to help Burke get custody, what if he helped his son in other ways, too?"

Faith turned in his arms. "Are you saying Mr. Thomas knew about Burke?"

How could anyone know about what Burke had done? Faith couldn't fathom it.

"All I know," Stefan said, "is my father smoothed over a few things he probably shouldn't have when I was a teenager. Fathers don't always make the best choices for their kids."

"Burke is a serial killer."

"And with his father gone, Burke doesn't have anyone to protect him anymore."

Ransom's words sent a chill through Faith.

Stefan squeezed her shoulders. "This could be an opportunity. Ransom may have the bigger hammer."

Not liking where this was going, Faith let out a long, slow breath. "I don't think—"

"This can work, Faith. Send your proof to CTC. All of it. Give them every piece of ammunition you have, and let them run with it. Without your father-in-law's influence, we have a chance to get Burke behind bars."

The energy and certainty in Stefan's voice reached into Faith's heart. Her mind whirled with unforeseen possibilities. For the first time in a long time, a small pinprick of hope filtered through the darkness.

Could she take the risk?

She met Stefan's gaze. She trusted Léon. And no matter what Stefan argued, his name changed nothing.

Faith placed her hand on his chest. "Okay," she whispered into the phone. "Let's end this."

Two HOURS LATER Stefan pressed the scanner button in Daniel's office, sending the last page of Faith's evidence to CTC. She sat on the sofa, her feet tucked under her, chewing on her nail as she watched each piece of paper feed through the scanner. He returned the last page to her, and she slipped it into the folder and secured it.

"That's everything," he said. Stefan's phone sounded and he pressed the speakerphone. "You're on with both of us, Ransom. What do you think?"

"I'm impressed," he said. "After the first batch I had Zane do some preliminary digging. Since Faith went into hiding, there's been one murder—of a woman who worked in Burke's office. Not to mention six women disappeared from the Dallas-Fort Worth and surrounding areas. All of them match the description."

"That's crazy."

"It gets worse. Three of the disappearances occurred in the last two weeks."

"He's escalating." Stefan couldn't stop the worry from his voice.

"It doesn't make sense." Faith rose from the sofa. "He killed after we fought, when he got angry with me. Why is he getting worse? I never meant for it to get worse."

"He was a murderer before he met you." Stefan forced her to meet his gaze. "This isn't your fault. You can't allow yourself to believe it is."

"Stefan's right, Faith." He paused for a moment. "I just learned another fact. Burke was with his father when he died."

Faith's eyes widened with shock.

"What was Burke's relationship with his father?" Ransom asked through the phone, his voice quiet.

Stefan recognized the moment Faith understood the implication of the question.

"You can't believe Burke killed his own father?"

"We need to consider whether or not this is a spree. If he's lost control, he'll take risks he wouldn't normally take, he'll do things he normally wouldn't do."

"Like make mistakes." A flood of curses circled Stefan's head.

"With too much collateral damage," Ransom added. "Faith, did Gerard control Burke?"

"Yes." Her voice croaked the words. She turned pale.

"Burke complained about the tight thumb he kept on the business, the money."

"Have Daniel do a psychological profile on Burke," Ransom ordered. "It wouldn't surprise me if there are murders back to his college days." The tapping of a keyboard sounded through the phone. "I have a few good friends in high places who I trust. Just hold tight. And stay safe. Don't give him an opportunity to find you. If he's on a spree, he's deadly. To anyone. And Stefan," he added. "Pick up."

The tone in his boss's voice froze Stefan. He tapped the screen and placed the phone to his ear. "What's wrong?"

Faith threaded her hand through his. He squeezed her fingers. With CTC's help, Faith and Zoe might end up with that happily ever after they wanted.

"Nothing's wrong exactly," Ransom said. "I debated whether or not to tell you, but you have a right to know before you leave Léon behind for good."

Stefan gripped the phone, bracing himself for bad news. His boss didn't prevaricate over good news. "Just say it."

"There's movement on the terrorist cell that put the hit out on you." Ransom lowered his voice. "They showed their hand too quickly when the Thomas photo went public. Your brother-in-law has a strong lead."

Stefan had been expecting a blip. He was surprised it had taken this long. Normally he would bail immediately and disappear until he could hook up with Annie, but one look at Faith made him pause. He had to think this through. "How solid a lead? Did they make it to the airport? Are they in Texas already?" His enemies bringing the fight here changed everything. No way would he risk Faith and Zoe. Or Daniel and his family.

"Logan's fairly certain they stopped them from boarding. They have three men in custody."

"Timeline?" Stefan asked.

"According to the itinerary, they would've made it to DFW in about twelve hours. Eighteen to reach Carder. If they had the location."

Stefan's neck muscles twitched. Terrorist groups were like roaches. Even if they appeared to be exterminated, they popped back up in greater numbers. "What if there were four? One could be on the way. You know better than most I can't count on hope."

"Logan's got them talking. The organization's been decimated by Katherine and Logan's anti-terrorism efforts. This is the best—if not the only—opportunity you'll get to come back from the dead."

Stefan couldn't think. If it were him alone, he might grab the opportunity with both hands, but he had others to consider. "I put a target on everyone around me."

"Give us twelve hours," Ransom countered. "It might be different this time."

"Don't bother." Stefan held Faith close. "Direct all your energies to helping Faith. I need to know she's safe."

"Twelve hours. Please." Ransom ended the call.

Knowing his luck, it probably wouldn't go well. Maybe plastic surgery. A more radical transformation?

He glanced down at Faith's worried expression. The modicum of hope he'd nurtured deep inside him, that maybe they could be together, that maybe they could find a future in some anonymous place with some anonymous name, had disintegrated.

"What did you just do?" She frowned at him. "Is everything okay?"

Stefan forced a confident smile to camouflage his worry. "Let's focus on you and Zoe staying safe. I'll worry about me later."

He texted Daniel and relayed Ransom's request, leaving the file on the desk.

"Talk to me," she said. "What's going on?"

"Catching Burke is Ransom's first priority. I made sure of that. It's going to be fine."

Faith sighed in resignation. "I guess that's it then."

Stefan didn't like the disappointment on her face, but he couldn't share the truth. She'd run right into danger, and he couldn't live with himself if something happened to her.

He wasn't ready to say good night—or goodbye. Still, he hesitated. When he said nothing, with heavy footsteps, she walked to the office door.

Before opening it, she turned to him. "Thank you, Stefan. For everything you've done. You didn't have to get involved, and you did." Her gaze warmed. "You reminded me that there are good people in the world."

Her footsteps faded up the stairs, leaving Stefan standing alone in Daniel and Raven's home. In that moment, he'd never felt more alone.

Nothing could be done about the situation until another lead popped. He trusted CTC to find one.

Tonight might be the last sleep he'd get for a while.

Heart heavy, he trudged up the stairs. Twelve hours from now he'd be forced to say goodbye, whatever happened.

Everything inside his body screamed not to leave her.

He had no choice. Neither of them did.

At the landing, he froze. Faith stood there, just outside the twins' room, looking beautiful and vulnerable and tempting.

She delicately closed the door and the lock snicked closed. "Zoe's asleep. Finally." Her lips turned down. "I'm worried about her. Something's not right. She usually bounces back from a pout before now."

He couldn't say a word so he touched her cheek. "Why aren't you closed safely behind that bedroom door, Faith?"

Her eyes flared with recognition. "I...I didn't do it on purpose." She tugged on his hand and pulled him down the hall to the guest room, closing and locking the door behind her.

Stefan swallowed deeply and covered her hand with his. "If things were different—"

"I know," she said softly. She cupped his face and pulled his lips down to hers. "Stefan."

When his real name whispered from her soft lips, he didn't resist. He couldn't.

He lowered his mouth to hers and wrapped her in his arms. All the wishes and hopes and dreams he'd been searching for the last several years came washing over him. They came alive in Faith's arms.

When Faith's hands tugged his shirt from his jeans, his heart thudded. He pulled back from her. "Are you sure?"

"I need you, Stefan. I need you now."

"Even if it's only for tonight? I don't know what tomorrow will bring."

"Tonight's all I'm asking for."

Stefan tugged his T-shirt off and slipped his hands under her blouse. She raised her arms and he pulled the shirt over her head. He touched the smooth skin at her waist before removing her bra and pressing her chest against his.

Skin to skin.

Her hands danced around his back. She lingered on the scars. He tensed under her touch, but she didn't shy away.

"How did you survive?" she whispered.

"Had no choice," he said, cupping her breast in his hand. Her nipple pebbled beneath his touch and she let out a low groan. "You don't have to touch them. I'd understand."

She hugged him tight. "They're part of you."

Stefan backed her toward the bed. He threw off the covers, scooped her into his arms and laid her on the cool sheets. His hands hovered over the button of her jeans, and with a flick of his fingers unfastened them.

He slipped his hand low on her belly and caressed the skin there. She shivered and he slipped the zipper down and removed the rest of her clothes.

Heart racing, he shucked his own jeans and followed her onto the bed, pressing her into the mattress.

His body throbbed with heat and he stared into her

brown eyes. She wrapped her legs around his hips and pulled him closer.

"Don't stop," she said into his ear. "Don't ever stop."

"Protection," Stefan said, his voice gravelly while he dug into the pocket of his jeans. He slipped on the condom and turned back to her.

With a groan, he joined them together.

Faith was like coming home. She wrapped her arms and legs tighter. With each movement she clung tighter. He reveled in her response, his body seeking out every untouched inch of her. Her nails scraped his shoulders, and he shuddered. Higher and higher they flew together.

Beneath him, Faith cried out in completion and he followed, relishing the pulsing caress of her body surrounding his. He had no wish to leave her or this bed ever again.

He'd found what he'd been looking for in Faith's arms. A strange peace settled over his heart and he shifted to his side. She followed him, plastered to his body.

She said no words, but they weren't needed.

Stefan stroked her hair and rested his chin on the top of her head.

He was complete with her in his arms. She was everything he wanted, everything he'd dreamed of, everything he'd hoped for.

And now he knew exactly what he'd be missing for the rest of his life.

STEFAN'S WARMTH SEEPED straight into Faith's soul. She cuddled against his strong, hard body and he squeezed her. His heart thudded against her ear. He'd been so tender, so loving, so giving.

That's what she'd been missing all these years.

Stefan had shown her the world when he'd loved her, as if he'd read her mind. He'd touched her places no one else had touched, made her feel things no one else had, made her want more. Made her want forever.

Except it was only one night. She'd promised.

She wanted to take the vow back.

Should she even ask? How could she? She'd been ready to run.

"What if…" Her voice trailed off.

His fingers toyed with her hair. "Don't," he said.

"Stay the night." She kissed his chest, letting her lips linger there for a few moments. "We have tonight."

"Even though in a few hours it'll be morning." He rose above her. "Tonight lasts until daylight."

Stefan lowered his lips to hers, taking her mouth. Faith couldn't stop the groan coming from deep within her belly.

"Tonight."

What she wouldn't give for tomorrow, over and over and over again.

THE SUN HAD been up for a while, but it was only seven in the morning. Burke had driven most of the night. He looked at his map and turned down a dirt road. A figure stood on the roadside. He pulled over and rolled down his window.

"Want a lift?"

Zoe smiled at her father, holding Catcher in her arms. "Hi, Daddy."

Chapter Eleven

A strange buzzing filtered through Faith's sleep-logged mind. She threw her arm to the side. It landed on a hard chest.

She blinked. Stefan. Her cheeks burned at the memory of last night right before a wave of sadness washed over her. One night was all he could promise.

Stefan passed her phone to her.

"No one calls me except Zoe," she said, her voice still husky with sleep. She pressed the phone's screen. "Hello."

"Good morning, Faith."

Her body went numb before she jerked to a sitting position. "Burke? How did you get this number?"

Stefan tilted the phone toward him and tapped the speaker icon.

"You didn't think you could hide from me forever, did you?"

Burke's voice sounded smug. The way it did when he knew he'd won. Her heart froze and she swallowed down the horrifying foreboding.

She clutched Stefan's hand. "What do you want?"

"Nothing." Burke's voice held a self-satisfied smile. "I have everything I want." A rustle filtered through the speaker. "Zoe, don't let the puppy run too far."

Faith's entire body froze in terror. "It can't be."

"Okay, Daddy," Zoe's voice called out.

Stefan jumped out of bed and raced from the room. Within a minute he returned. "She's gone," he mouthed. "And a puppy's missing."

"How?" Faith asked. How had he found them?

"You don't know your daughter as well as you thought," Burke taunted. "Zoe called me. She needed to be rescued. Remember when I rescued you, Faith? You let me down. I'm going to make certain Zoe can't betray me."

His words strangled her breath. Faith's mind whirled, remembering everything Ransom had said. "Please, Burke—"

"Shut up, Faith. Here's the way it's going to work. I have Zoe. We're done with custody. If you want to see *my* daughter again, I'll let you say goodbye to her. Then you can go wherever you want, but Zoe is mine. No negotiations."

Faith choked back a sob. "Please—"

"Don't bother begging. Drive toward the Guadalupe Mountains. I'll text you instructions along the way. Oh, and Faith, come alone. Whoever you're sleeping with, he'll just make me angry. Maybe you won't get to see Zoe after all."

The phone went dead.

Faith wrapped a robe around her nude body and stood. "She called him? How? How did this happen?"

Stefan shook his head. "Daniel and Raven are working on the twins in the kitchen. Your instincts were right yesterday."

"I ignored my gut because I wanted to spend time with you." Faith hugged her arms. "I knew something was off with Zoe."

He placed his hands on her shoulders. "This isn't your fault. It's Burke's. You couldn't have known. You're not psychic."

"I'm a mom. I'm supposed to know when my child is thinking of doing something like this." She rubbed her eyes. "Why would Zoe call him?"

"One way to find out."

They dressed quickly and walked down the hall to the kitchen. Daniel and Raven faced two solemn little girls.

Raven had her hands on her hips. "Where did this plan come from?"

Christina swung her feet back and forth. Hope refused to meet her parents' gaze.

Faith walked over to the table and knelt in front of the twins. "I'm worried about Zoe, girls. I need to know why she left."

The twins met each other's gazes. Hope gave Christina a quick nod.

"Zoe was really mad. She wanted to go home so she could play baseball with Danny and have a backyard for Catcher. You told her if Catcher had a backyard, she could keep him. So she called her dad."

"Not on my phone," Faith said.

"On mine." Raven passed over the cell. "They

called late last night. She snuck out at daylight and took Catcher with her. The girls turned off the security system."

Daniel placed his hands on his hips. "You two are in big trouble. Zoe's mom is scared for her."

"But she's with her daddy. Daddies take care of you," Hope said.

"Not all daddies," Daniel said quietly. "Go on. You're grounded. No puppies today. No games. Your mother will come up with a list of chores. Until then, I want you sitting quietly in your room."

"Yes, Daddy," they said together and walked out of the kitchen, heads held low.

Daniel faced Faith. "I'm so sorry."

"It's not their fault. It's mine. I didn't know how to tell Zoe about her father, and why we were hiding. She still trusts him because of me." Faith rubbed her eyes. She had no idea what Burke would do. "I need a car to rendezvous with my ex. Maybe I can convince him—"

"You're not going alone. I'm coming with you," Stefan interjected.

She shook her head. "He said I should come alone."

"He's a killer."

Faith whirled on him. "You think I don't know that? I have to do whatever it takes to keep Zoe safe."

Stefan held her hands in his and squeezed until she met his gaze. "We'll get Zoe back, but you can't do this alone, Faith. You don't have to. You have me." He pulled her in his arms and held her close. "We can do this smart. I'll follow you. We'll set up a tracker on your phone. You'll never be alone. I promise."

"It's not right to put you in danger," she whispered. "It's not right."

He smiled at her. "It's what Léon Royce does."

"And Stefan?"

"Stefan protects the ones he cares about most. No matter the cost."

THE CRAGGY ROCKS of the Guadalupe Mountains could hide a multitude of sins. The crevices might come in handy today. Burke hiked past the trail and scanned the rugged terrain. Too many hiding places here. This wasn't the right place for his rendezvous with Faith. He checked the first possibility off his list.

"Daddy, I'm tired," Zoe whined behind him.

He gritted his teeth to keep himself from yelling at her. "Not much farther."

"Catcher is tired, too."

He glanced at Orren. "If this is going to work, I need her away from the meeting."

Orren nodded. "We could hole up in a cave."

Burke pulled out a series of photos from his bag. The satellite image showed an old miner's shack just over that ridge. "Take her there. It's far enough away she won't hear anything, and she can't call out."

The man nodded. Burke pulled out his canteen and knelt in front of Zoe.

"I need you to be a big girl. I have to meet someone and it's far away. Orren is going to take you to a place where you and your puppy can rest, okay?"

"But I don't know him," she said with a frown at Orren. "I want to be with you, Daddy. You promised."

Burke gritted his teeth to hold back his instincts. He fought against the inclination to shut her up. His skin prickled with irritation.

"Zoe, we're going to be together all the time soon. Just do this for me, honey? Then we'll go back to my house and your puppy can have a big yard."

She crossed her arms in front of her and glared.

"I thought you were brave. Was I wrong?" Burke winced at the whining in his voice.

"I'm not scared. I'm tired and hungry. Mom wouldn't make me wait to have my breakfast."

Burke's nails dug into the heel of his hand. He couldn't lose control. "Can you be brave for me and climb some more? Then you can have a snack."

"I guess." Zoe sighed, cuddling the puppy in her arms.

"Let me have the puppy," he said.

She backed away.

"I'm going to put him in your backpack, honey. That's all."

Reluctantly, Zoe let him.

He slipped the backpack on her shoulders. "Follow Orren, sweetie." Zoe trudged after the man. As they reached the top of the hill, she looked back at Burke.

He waved at her until she no longer turned around. Finally.

With his daughter out of the way, he could get down to business. He'd know soon enough if paying for the high-def photos via drone surveillance had been worth the money.

He veered toward a group of pines. He pushed

through the grove and came to a clearing. His heart-
beat picked up a bit. The prickles snaked down his
spine. He scanned the perimeter and his gaze stopped
at a spot where a strange gap appeared between the
rock formations. He walked toward the fissure and
peered over the side.

His heart leaped. He couldn't even make out the
bottom of the ravine.

Perfect. Nowhere for Faith to run. All he had to do
would be to maneuver Faith toward the edge. No one
would ever find her.

THE DRIVE TO the base of the Guadalupe Mountains took
far too long. Each mile, Stefan's mind lingered on Zoe
in the hands of a madman. He'd orchestrated his share
of drop-offs, but nothing compared to this. Usually, his
partner had been trained, and was as deadly with any
weapon as he was. Faith didn't have those skills, but
she had more heart than he'd ever seen.

She sat next to him, stiff and unyielding, because
she blamed herself.

He understood, because he felt the same way for
not protecting Zoe. He'd promised. What could either
of them say?

So, they said nothing.

They sped past the latest mile marker. The road was
deserted. Not many frequented this side of the Guadalupe Mountains National Park, making it a great
meet site. The mountains could be brutal, and Burke
had chosen this location for a reason. People disappeared. Permanently.

Stefan knew Faith's ex had set a trap. She just hadn't realized it yet.

She would.

"We're going to find her," Stefan repeated.

"I can't believe anything else, but…" Faith stared out the window. "My heart's breaking. Zoe possesses this light inside her. That trust you have when you're a kid. I don't want her to lose it, and I don't know how to stop it from happening."

He tucked her hand in his and squeezed. She didn't pull away, to his surprise. "You can't protect her from the truth, Faith."

"I can want to."

He caressed her palm with his thumb, and she leaned her head back against the car seat. His sidelong glance revealed the tension around her mouth, the stark paleness of her face.

"What's Burke's plan?" she asked, eyes still closed.

Stefan didn't want to tell her, but she had to be ready. "He knows you'll never let Zoe go willingly and with his father dead, he can't risk you causing him any trouble."

"He wants me gone," she said, "so he forces me to come out here alone, in the middle of nowhere." She paused for a few seconds before her jaw tightened. "He doesn't plan on letting me leave these mountains, does he?"

"That would be my guess." Stefan tightened his grip on her. "He believes you don't have help. That you're alone. He doesn't know what you know or how strong you are, Faith. He won't get what he wants. We'll make certain of that."

"I'm afraid for Zoe." Faith swallowed. "Would he hurt her?"

Stefan didn't want to answer. "Do you think Burke's capable of love?"

He wouldn't mention Daniel's initial opinion, that Burke possessed antisocial personality disorder. Stefan preferred the term *sociopath*. Fewer syllables.

Faith shifted in her seat. "If he loves anyone, it might be his mother. He's devoted to her. And Burke's mother loves Zoe."

"Interesting." Stefan mulled the new information. "If he's focused on his mother being happy and occupied—and ignorant to his true nature—he might use Zoe. Without you in the way, his mother takes care of Zoe and he has a clear field to kill whenever he wants. As long as he doesn't get caught."

"Even if something happens to me, he'll go to prison." She gripped his shirt. "You promised."

"Ransom called in a few favors in the state attorney general's office. From what I hear, more than one official was trying to cover their tracks. They're running. Burke doesn't know it yet, but he's trapped with no way out."

"And what happens when he realizes I've turned my evidence over to the authorities?"

"We get Zoe out of there before he knows."

Burke would become a trapped animal. A cornered serial killer wasn't someone Stefan wanted to try to reason with.

His phone rang and he tapped the screen.

"You're nearing the turnoff," Ransom announced over the speakerphone. "Zane's cast a little computer voodoo. We've got Faith's phone on a satellite tracker. We'll be able to ping her location anywhere, as long as it doesn't get too cloudy."

The Guadalupe Mountains loomed ahead, and he veered the vehicle toward the hiking trail.

"What about backup?" Stefan asked.

"Sheriff Galloway will be your closest resource. I'll have a helicopter on standby in Trouble, Texas, in an hour. They'll be able to reach you in less than thirty minutes. The rest of the team is on their way, but they're two-plus hours out. Unless you can delay."

"No can do." Stefan cleared his throat. "They didn't have to drop everything."

"You've saved their lives more than once. You're part of CTC. You always will be. No matter what happens. We're family. Besides, I couldn't stop them trying."

With that, Ransom ended the call.

"You have good friends," Faith said.

"They have my back." Stefan eyed his odometer. They should be getting close.

Sure enough, two vehicles sat off to the side of the road. He pulled next to the sheriff's car, behind a second SUV.

Sheriff Garrett Galloway exited his car and walked around to the side. Stefan rolled down his window, and Garrett dropped the keys into his hand. "Gassed and ready," he said.

"Thanks, Sheriff."

"I'm taking a side route. I'll be nearby. Just send up a smoke signal. I'll get there as quickly as I can."

Stefan exited the SUV, leaving it running. He met Faith's gaze. She looked scared, but determined.

"You won't be alone," he said.

She slid into the driver's side. "I know."

Stefan leaned into the open window, grabbed her face and kissed her. "I promise. Come nightfall, Zoe will be back with you."

She smiled weakly. "I know."

THE WEST TEXAS road snaked across the desert with shrub bushes peppering the landscape. Faith's fingers ached from her grip on the steering wheel. She was close to the base of the large mountains.

Burke could very well kill her the moment she arrived. She knew that. Stefan knew that. The only thing that gave Faith comfort was the fact that Stefan would see to it that Zoe was safe.

She pulled over to the mile marker that Burke had mentioned in his last text. The hot sun pounded her through the windshield. She waited. And waited.

Moments ticked by. Fifteen minutes. A half hour.

Where was he?

She wished she knew where Stefan was located. She believed he was watching. She had to believe it.

Finally, a truck pulled over. An old man looked at her from the driver's side.

"You Faith?" he asked.

She nodded.

"Your husband said he's waiting for you at the mile two marker of the Guadalupe Peak Trail."

"Where is that?"

"Up fifteen miles. Veer to the right. You'll see a small visitor's center. There's a trail that leads up toward Guadalupe Peak. It'll take a while to walk, but you'll find him."

The man cleared his throat. "He told me your cell phone doesn't work. He wants you to give it to me."

"What?"

"He said you have to give your cell phone to me or you won't be able to meet him." The guy stroked his beard. "Seemed a bit weird to me, but he wants us to trade phones."

She forced a smile. Was he watching? She glanced behind her. She didn't have a choice. At least if Stefan followed her phone, he'd get the information of where she'd gone.

She handed the phone over and the old man dropped an old flip-style cell in her hand.

"Good luck." He shuffled toward his vehicle.

Faith bit her lip. "Ummm…what did the man who gave you the directions look like?"

"Don't you know your own husband?"

What was she supposed to say to that?

"Can't be too careful these days."

"Brown hair. Scar on his face."

In other words, not Burke. He'd left nothing to tie him to her. No witnesses. And she had no way to contact Stefan, unless she used Burke's phone. Could she risk it?

Before she could respond, the phone rang.

"You received the instructions?" Burke asked.

"Yes. Is Zoe okay?"

"Of course. Why wouldn't she be? Now drive."

The old man had heaved himself into his truck and his engine gunned to life.

She pulled off the highway. "What now?"

"Follow his instructions." Burke paused. "And Faith. Don't detour, don't contact anyone. I'll know. This is between you and me, no one else. I need your promise."

A promise used to mean something in their marriage. Faith had never broken her word to Burke. This would be the first time. "I promise."

"Excellent."

A loud explosion pierced the sky. Faith's hands jerked the steering wheel. Behind her a pillow of black smoke erupted into the sky.

"Throw the phone out of the car. Now."

Oh, God. Had Burke killed the old man?

"I'll only say this once more. Get rid of the phone. If you're not at the mile marker in thirty minutes, you'll be too late," Burke said. "You'll never see Zoe again."

He was watching. Where was he? Not that it mattered.

She couldn't believe he'd blown up the car. The poor man. And her phone was destroyed.

Which meant Stefan had no way to track her.

She tossed Burke's phone along with an earring out of the car. She drove on the side of the road, hoping Stefan or Garrett or someone might see which direction she was going.

The odometer ticked away the miles. Every couple miles she tossed something else out of the car. Another earring; a lipstick, anything she could find that he'd be able to recognize as possibly hers. After thirteen miles, her entire body reminded her of a tightly wound rubber band ready to break. She tossed out a hair tie of Zoe's just as she turned off to the visitor's center.

Around her, shrub bushes and pine trees lined the building. She didn't go inside. Why bother? There were no cars, no people, no nothing.

Deserted. No one to see her enter the national park. She glanced at her watch. She was running out of time. Uncertain if Stefan had seen any of her signs, she had to trust him and his ability.

A wooden sign delineated the trail's beginning. She could make an arrow with rocks, but it would be obvious. If Burke brought her back this way, he'd know what she was doing. Instead, she used her foot to scratch an arrow in the dirt.

She started up the trail, walking slowly, digging into a baggie of Zoe's clips and elastics she kept in her purse, dropping them like a trail of breadcrumbs. If Stefan were looking for her, he'd know which direction to head.

About a quarter mile into the walk she made a show of slipping on the trail to offer another sign, then struggled to get back up. She brushed off her pants and hiked another mile. Fifteen minutes later, she rounded a curve in the trail.

A figure stood at the top of the hill. She hadn't seen

him in months. Just the sight of him made her gut twist in revulsion.

Burke waited for her, arms crossed, his dark hair perfectly slicked back, his khaki pants ironed with a stiff crease, and his button-down starched just as he preferred. Perfect. Cool, composed and calm.

Who went hiking dressed like that? A crazy serial killer, that's who.

Faith stared at him, trying to see behind him.

"Where's Zoe?"

Burke grinned, a smile that at one time had blinded her to the deadness behind his eyes.

"She's not here." He raised his hand. "Before you start, she's safe. I decided you and I should have a reunion first. Just the two of us. We have a few things to discuss."

Chapter Twelve

This place was worse than the ugly house her mom had made her stay in. Zoe took Catcher out of her backpack. The puppy wriggled in her arms. She hugged his soft fur and buried her face deep. She wanted her mom.

The man—Orren was his name—had practically dragged her up the mountain. Her father shouldn't have made her go away. Not with this man.

Zoe frowned at the tall figure glaring at her. He didn't like being stuck in this wooden hut, either.

Catcher whined in her arms and nibbled at her finger.

"Ouch," she muttered. "Your teeth are sharp."

"Keep the dog quiet," the man rumbled in a low voice.

"He's just a baby."

Orren muttered something under his breath. "Burke has lost it." He paced back and forth like Zoe's mom did when she was worried.

"What do we do now?" Zoe asked.

"None of your business. Just sit on the floor and stay quiet. Your dad will be here soon."

"You were supposed to give us something to eat," Zoe said.

He whipped around and growled at her, like a wolf. "Shut up and sit down or you'll be sorry."

Catcher wiggled in her arms and jumped out of them. The puppy charged at Orren with a loud yip. The high-pitched bark hurt Zoe's ears.

Orren pulled a big gun out of his pants—just like on television. He pointed it at Catcher. "Shut up, dog!"

"No, you can't hurt him." Zoe ran over and grabbed the man's arm.

"That dog will ruin everything," the man said, shaking Zoe off. "I'm not losing my payday. Not for a mutt."

He kicked out at Catcher. Zoe gasped and dove for the puppy. The man's boot hit her shoulder, but Catcher didn't get hurt.

Zoe's back throbbed. Orren's face had turned red. He looked real mad. She wasn't staying here.

With a shout, she scooped up the puppy. The man lunged for her. No way would she let him hurt Catcher.

Zoe scooted backward across the old wood floor. Orren loomed over her, his arms reaching for her like a monster. She kept scooching until she caught sight of a missing board that left a gap in the side of the shack. She wasn't staying here. She had to find her daddy. Orren wasn't nice. He was bad.

He bent over close. She held her breath, hugged Catcher and squeezed through the opening.

Orren yelled a very bad word. "Kid! Come back here."

Zoe didn't look back. She held on tight to Catcher and ran as fast as she could.

The man slammed open the front door. "Stop, kid. Your dad will be mad. You can't run away."

No way was Zoe answering him. She remembered what Léon had taught her. She darted between some big trees and bushes and searched for a place to hide. A wall of rocks shot up into the sky. She squinted through all the grass and saw a small cave just at the bottom.

The man's huge footsteps were chasing her. They pounded somewhere behind her. She couldn't outrun him, even if she was faster than Danny. Orren was a grown-up.

She darted into the hole and took a few steps inside. It curved around. Her eyes widened. The room got really big and very dark. She held Catcher tight.

"Go inside my backpack, Catcher. I need both hands."

She couldn't lose him or she'd never find him in this scary place. He whimpered, but settled in okay. She slipped the backpack on and took a step forward.

The ground below her crumbled and disappeared.

"Mommy!"

Smoke billowed into the sky from the explosion. The blast had stopped Stefan's heart. His SUV skidded up to a blazing truck in the middle of the road. He slammed on the brakes. The fire charred the metal and his entire body went numb.

"You're sure this is the last location of her phone?" He could barely enunciate the words.

"Yeah." Ransom's voice was solemn. "Then we lost all signal."

"What's Faith's phone doing in a truck?"

He didn't want to think, didn't want to move. His mind kept flashing to another burned-out home. The Jennings house. He'd lost all of them, including the bastard who'd blown them up. Jenny and her kids. They hadn't deserved to die, and he'd been too late to stop it.

Shoving the past out of his mind, he stepped closer. A wall of heat slammed at him. This wasn't her vehicle. It couldn't be her.

He squinted at the charred body inside and his eyes centered on the metal socket in the man's shoulder.

"Not Faith."

His knees shook and he stumbled back to his car. He sucked in a couple of deep breaths. Their plan had gone to hell.

"It's not her," he said, his voice choked. He slammed his fist into the side of the vehicle.

"Thank God." Ransom barked some orders on his side of the phone. "We'll trace the signal backward as far as we can."

"I promised her, Ransom. I promised her I'd keep them safe."

"We'll find them."

Ransom's words were a jumbled mess. Stefan's head swirled with fury. Burke had done this. Covering his tracks. He had to track her down.

"...stopped at mile marker twelve," Ransom said through the phone. "The phone reversed direction. We assumed he was testing for a tail."

"I'm headed for the mile marker where she stopped. Call everyone in. We've got to find her."

Stefan drove down the deserted West Texas road like he'd entered Le Mans. When the marker was ten feet ahead of him, he stopped. Faith's car wasn't in sight.

He strode down the road, searching for anything out of place. A glint of silver caught his eye.

An old flip phone. And something else next to it.

His breath caught. He knelt down and picked up a gold hoop earring and squeezed it tight. Oh, yeah, baby.

She'd been wearing these the day they'd met at the library. She'd never taken them off, probably because they were her only pair. She'd been here. He scanned the gravel at the edge of the road.

One thing about Faith, she could think on her feet. He walked on the side of the road for a half mile.

The other earring gleamed from the black tar.

He scooped it up, activated his phone and ran back to the SUV. "She's headed toward the mountains. She left me a damn trail of breadcrumbs.

"Call Daniel. Have him bring Trouble. We might need the dog if I can't find her fast."

Stefan jumped in and started toward the mountains. Every mile he caught sight of a small clue. When he saw the lipstick he practically cheered.

"I'll find you, Faith. I promise."

He drove along the side of the road and paused at an obvious turnoff, but he didn't see any signs of recent activity or of a car turning off. The weeds growing in the middle of the road hadn't been disturbed.

He was taking a chance, but Faith was smart. If she could, she'd guide him. That was a big *if.* Maybe

Burke had stopped her. Maybe he'd forced her into the back seat.

Shoving the worst case into the recesses of his mind, Stefan tried to treat this like any other mission, except it wasn't. He'd fallen for Faith. More and harder than he'd ever imagined. Not to mention Zoe. That little girl held his heart in her baseball glove.

After a couple miles of nothing, he almost stopped. Should he retrace his steps? Maybe try that turn? His foot tapped the brakes just as a glint shined in the road ahead.

A hundred feet later he hit pay dirt. A compact. He'd seen her use it when they'd been driving to his campsite.

He could breathe again.

Man, she was tough.

Another couple miles and a white SUV appeared abandoned near a small building. Stefan palmed his weapon and slowly pulled up to the vehicle. He peered into the back and called Ransom. "She left her car at the base of Guadalupe Peak Trail. She's not here, but she started hiking."

"How far behind her do you think you are?"

Stefan knelt down beside the arrow she'd scratched into the hiking trail and the pattern of grass and oxidation beneath her steps. "Too long. No sign of a second set of prints, though. She was alone."

"The team is still an hour away. Unless you want Garrett to fly in on the chopper."

"I don't want him spooked until I'm in position.

Give me a half hour. If you don't hear from me, send in the cavalry."

"You got it." Ransom paused. "And Stefan. Don't get dead."

"Will do."

Stefan ended the call and trudged up the trail, searching for any more signs from Faith. Every so often he'd pick up a tie for Zoe's hair, a button. At the top of a hill two miles in he stopped. A man's shoe print. Size eleven.

Burke.

Stefan clutched his weapon and followed the trail until the footprints ended. He swept the area of pinyon pine and Southwestern white pine on each side.

Above him, thunder cracked across the afternoon sky. Black clouds hovered over the mountain, streaks of gray dropped to earth. A hell of a summer storm high up, which meant flash floods heading down.

"Where's Zoe, Burke?"

Faith's shout pierced the air from Stefan's left. He raced toward the sound and burst into a clearing.

Burke hovered over Faith. Blood zigzagged across her forehead.

Stefan raised his gun.

"You move, and you're a dead man." He glanced at the bruise darkening Faith's cheek. "Hell, I may just kill you anyway."

Faith scrambled to her feet and stood between Stefan and Burke, holding her hands up.

Stefan froze. "What are you doing?"

She swiped her face and the blood smeared across

her forehead. "Zoe's not here and Burke's the only one
who knows where she is."

STORM CLOUDS COVERED the sun. The sky had turned
angry and violent.

Faith stared at Stefan's weapon. Behind her, Burke
let out a curse and grabbed Faith around the waist. He
plastered her to his body. Cold metal pressed across
her throat. She glanced down. He held a knife against
her skin.

"Throw your weapon down or she dies."

"Burke. You can't do this."

"Of course I can," he said. "Who's going to stop me?
You? My father?" Burke chuckled. "Father's dead and
can't protect you any longer. Mother doesn't know a
thing. And you, you're going to end up at the bottom
of that gorge along with your lover. If they ever do find
you, they'll assume you both died in a lover's quarrel.
All the better for me."

"Burke, Zoe needs me."

He scoffed. "Zoe needs a woman to raise her who
knows what it means to be a woman. You, you're nothing. I was a fool for thinking you could ever learn to
be my consort."

She struggled against his tight grip, but his grip only
tightened. "Have to tie up all the loose ends. Then life
will be perfect again."

He really was insane.

Burke dragged her to the right. Stefan followed step
for step.

"Please, Burke. Where is Zoe?" she begged.

"There's no need for you to know. You don't get to see her again. She's mine. Didn't I tell you that?"

"She's alone, afraid. Please. She's your daughter."

Faith wanted to duck down, let Stefan do what he was obviously willing to do, but she couldn't. What if they were unable to find Zoe?

Burke chuckled. "Oh, she's not alone. If I don't come back, he'll take Zoe away. You'll never see her again."

He jerked her toward rocks at the edge of the clearing, using her as a shield against Stefan.

"You don't have to do this," Stefan said quietly. "We just want Zoe to be safe. We can all walk away."

Burke shook his head. "Father was right about one thing. No loose ends is the only way."

Stefan chuckled. "You don't believe that, do you? We know all about you, Burke. Faith figured out your little hobby. Why else do you think she ran away?"

Burke gripped her even tighter. "It's not possible."

"Faith is smart and resourceful. She figured out your twisted game, and she gave me the file."

Burke gripped Faith's throat and squeezed. She gasped for air. "You're lying."

"Cassandra. Allison. Mary Ann, Brittany, Alexandra. Do those names sound familiar?"

With each name, Burke's grip tightened. His hands shook. Faith could feel the fury. Spots circled in front of her eyes.

"We know." Stefan glanced at his watch. "In fact, as we speak, a very influential member of the state attorney general's staff is perusing the documents right now. It's over, Burke. Your best move is to let Faith go and tell us where to find Zoe. If you do that, I'll put in a good word for you."

"No. Not possible."

Faith held her breath. Burke had stopped moving. He'd turned slightly. She met Stefan's gaze. He gave a slight nod of his head toward the ground. Did he want her to try to get away?

Burke bore down on her throat again. "I don't believe you. Father covered my tracks. I killed him and the men who helped him. No one's left. No one can prove anything." Burke pulled out a knife from behind his back. "Except you."

"Now!" Stefan shouted.

Faith wrenched her body forward, but she couldn't break Burke's hold. The knife sliced her skin. Warm fluid trickled down her neck.

She tumbled to the ground. A loud gunshot echoed through the woods. Faith's gaze flew at the noise. Stefan held the gun in his hand.

Burke screamed. He dropped the knife. One arm hung limp at his side. Blood dripped down his arm. He stared at Stefan in shock.

"You shot me?"

"Be thankful I wasn't aiming at your head. Now where is Zoe?"

Burke shook his head. "This isn't the plan."

His hand jerked. He twisted, looked at Faith and then behind her. "This is all your fault. Everything is your fault," he screamed. "You were supposed to be perfect for me. You were supposed to replace my true love. My Heather."

He gripped her arm with his good hand and dragged her backward. She tried to wrench away, but she couldn't escape his grip.

"Give it up, Burke. It's over," Stefan said.

"It's not over," he said. "Not until I have control."

He shouted out a curse and rammed her with his body. She stumbled toward the rocks.

Stefan let out a loud curse and rushed toward them.

His eyes wild and desperate, he lunged at Faith. She rolled to her side to avoid him. He pitched forward and let out a loud yell.

"Move!" Stefan yelled.

Faith lurched to her left. Burke tripped and couldn't regain his step. He hurtled over the cliff.

"No!" Faith shouted. "Zoe!"

DIRT RAINED DOWN on Zoe. She blinked up at the hole she'd fallen through. No way she was climbing out that way.

"Damn it, kid. Your dad's gonna kill me. Wait right there."

The puppy squirmed in her backpack. She peeked inside, but she could barely see in the dark. "You okay, Catcher?"

She nuzzled the dog. A flash brightened the hole she'd fallen into. Thunder clapped and echoed.

"We're not getting out that way," she whispered. "And I'm not waiting around for that bad man to hurt you." She dug into the pocket of her backpack. "Stefan gave me this." She pulled the mini flashlight out in triumph.

A rope dropped down through the hole in the ceiling.

Zoe swung on her knapsack and flipped on the flashlight. There were railroad tracks on the floor of the cave. It was a very small train. Her mom had taken her onto a big train once. She swept the flashlight around. No way would that train fit in this cave.

A glint blinked at her through the light. She tiptoed through the cave. A big pile of dirt had come down. "Look, Catcher. Another tunnel."

She peered around the mound that was twice as tall as she was. A bunch of shiny gold rocks were piled high in a corner. She picked one up that was the size of a baseball. It was way heavier than her ball.

"Cool." She stuffed it into her backpack with Catcher.

A loud curse echoed through the cave. She whirled around. The man's feet came through the hole. "We gotta go."

She hesitated. There were two tunnels. "Which one, Catcher?"

Zoe squinted down the one with the yellow rocks. Dirt sprinkled down from the ceiling. The other one was bigger. Catcher whined.

"I think you're right," she said. "Let's go that way, boy."

"Kid. You better stay right there," the man shouted.

She'd waited too long. Zoe took off running beside the railroad track. A trickle of water followed her.

Her heart beat fast. Her pants for breath echoed against the rocks around her.

"Kid! Stop. There's a flash flood coming."

She didn't know what he was talking about, but she knew she couldn't trust him.

A loud rumble sounded behind her. Rocks came down. The man shouted. Zoe didn't care. She kept running, the light from her flashlight bobbing in the dark.

"Kid. Stop!"

She glanced over her shoulder. He was gaining on her. A huge wall of rocks rumbled down behind him. Water rushed through a small hole at the side. She looked down at her feet. The whole cave was wet. Zoe stared into the blackness ahead of her. She was trapped. There was nowhere to go.

Chapter Thirteen

Through the sprinkling rain Stefan stared over the side of the cliff. He couldn't see Burke's body, but no one could have survived a fall hundreds of feet down. He turned to Faith. She sat on the ground, her eyes wide with shock.

"Is he—?"

Stefan nodded and crouched beside her. He pulled her into his arms. Her nails bit into his skin. "Zoe."

"We'll find her."

He helped her to her feet. "Let me look at your neck."

She slapped his hand away. "I'm fine."

The cut wasn't deep, but still oozing. He tore a strip from his T-shirt and pressed it against the wound. "This should stop the bleeding."

"Zoe!" Faith shouted, while he tied the makeshift bandage around her neck.

"Don't call out to her," he said. "You heard Burke. Someone's with her."

"Then how will we find her?"

He glanced around the clearing. The trees just to the northwest were disturbed. "This way," he said.

"Are you sure?"

"As much as I can be." He took her hand and led her out of the clearing.

She glanced back to the cliff.

"We'll find his body. After we find Zoe," he said.

Thunder growled ahead of them. Angry clouds hovered over the mountain. "The water'll start coming through the canyons soon," he said. "Looks like a huge rainstorm up there."

"Zoe doesn't know anything about flash floods. We've got to find her."

Stefan stared at the ground. The wind and rain would compromise any trail he might have followed if they didn't find her soon.

The sky darkened even more. Stefan stopped. The mountains were too quiet. He could only make out the sound of the wind through the branches and the pattering rain. No Zoe. No sounds of human activity at all.

He looked around him.

"She's with some kidnapper. What if he—"

He recognized the panic in her voice. He understood, but they had to stay focused. "Burke's a powerful employer. The guy doesn't know Burke's dead. He has to keep Zoe safe."

Faith nodded. "Right. Janice loves Zoe. He'll want her safe."

Stefan didn't mention Burke's erratic behavior. Faith knew. They both did.

Before long, the signs Stefan had been following had disappeared.

Stefan walked a few steps forward. He bent down, then craned his neck to look back the way they'd come.

"You don't know which way, do you?" Faith said. "What are we going to do?" She rubbed her arms quickly.

Stefan pulled her close. She was chilled to the bone. "Burke wouldn't have wanted her too far."

"But maybe far enough not to be heard? Or to hear him."

"Exactly." Stefan grabbed his sat phone and verified his location. Thank God for CTC.

"Are you okay?" Ransom asked.

"Burke's dead. He's hidden Zoe. Who knows these mountains?"

"Sheriff Galloway." Ransom didn't hesitate. "He's on his way. About thirty minutes from your location."

"Can you patch me through to him?"

"Want me to send the chopper?"

"We need everyone you can spare, but it's raining in the mountains. Warn them about flash floods."

Ransom let out a curse. "I'll patch you through to Garrett."

Faith plastered herself against Stefan. He wrapped his arm around her. "We've got help."

She gave him a stiff nod.

"Galloway."

"This is Léon. We've got a missing child—"

"Ransom filled me in. I'm heading your way."

"The guy hid his daughter out here somewhere. I need likely locations. The weather obscured any signs."

Stefan fed Garrett his GPS coordinates. Paper rustling filtered through the phone. "Okay, I'm looking at the map."

"There are a lot of old mine shafts," Garrett said. "They're not safe, though."

The phone went silent. "This looks interesting. There's an old hunting cabin a mile or so northwest from your current location."

Stefan could have cheered. "Thanks, Garrett. I'll be in touch."

"We'll send searchers up your way. Good luck."

Stefan ended the call. "This way," he said, and led her up another hill.

A quarter mile in, the rain let up, but thunder and lightning still hid the top of the mountains.

He fingered a broken branch. "Someone came this way, and not that long ago." He turned to Faith. "We're headed in the right direction."

"I want to call for her," Faith muttered. She dug her hand into his arm. "I want her to know we're coming for her."

"You can't."

Stefan could tell Faith was near her breaking point when they reached the cabin. It was nestled back in the woods. Stefan pulled out his weapon. He slowly turned the doorknob and shoved into the one-room shack.

Empty.

Faith turned to Stefan, her eyes devastated. "Where is she?"

ZOE TOOK A step back, her foot sloshing through cold water. The puppy whimpered from her backpack. The yellow rock weighed it down.

She shined the light through the rocks. The side of the man's face was bleeding. He looked really mad.

"You've killed us, kid," he growled.

Water streamed behind him. It started getting deeper and deeper.

He pushed aside the rocks and came closer and closer. Zoe didn't wait for him to catch her. She whirled around and ran.

"Nowhere to go, kid. I'm gonna to do what Burke was too scared to do. Before I die, you're dead."

Zoe heaved forward. She tried to run, but the water was at her knees now. She lifted her legs, but she couldn't get any traction. The water pushed her forward. Soon it was up to her waist. The flashlight slipped through her wet hands and blinked off.

Dark surrounded her. Rushing water carried her forward in the small cave. She blinked. The backpack weighed her down. Catcher barked at her. Her teeth chattered.

This wasn't good.

The man behind her sloshed closer. She rounded a curve and blinked. A little twinkle of light shone from one end, like a star in the rock.

She headed toward it.

"Got you," the man growled.

His hands gripped her shirt. She squirmed, but he had her. The water climbed higher.

The man held her down, below the water. She couldn't breathe. The water shoved her forward and suddenly she was free. She lifted her head and sucked in a deep breath.

"Damn it," he groaned. He floated close to the ceiling. Blood dripped from his head.

Zoe only had one chance. She let the water carry her toward the hole with the light. It wasn't very big.

She pulled herself up. "Don't worry, Catcher. We're almost safe," she panted.

Something grabbed at her foot.

"Oh, no you don't."

THE EMPTY CABIN sucked all the life out of Faith. Her gaze swept the floor.

"Someone's been here recently," Stefan said.

A glint of string caught Faith's attention. "Zoe," she said, picking up the red tie. "This was on her backpack."

Stefan tilted his head. "There's a trail across the floor." He grinned. "That feisty little sweetheart." He glanced over at Faith.

"She escaped. Zoe ran away. Come on," he called.

They ran through the back door. Stefan headed for the edge of the clearing. "Broken branches," he said.

Faith raced after him. The wind had slowed down. She could even hear the songs of a few birds.

A high-pitched yip pierced the air.

"Stop," Stefan said.

The yip sounded again.

"The dog," Faith shouted. The dog she'd denied Zoe. They ran toward the noise.

"Let me go!" Zoe shouted.

"Zoe!" Faith yelled. Her legs pumped harder as she scrambled over the rocks. They rounded a bend and she gasped.

Zoe's torso came out of a hole in the rocks and water poured out on either side. Her orange backpack lay on the ground. Catcher raced around in circles, yipping at Zoe.

"Mommy. Help. I'm stuck."

Stefan positioned himself in front of her. "I'm going first. We don't know where our friend is."

Faith scrambled over the rocks behind him.

"Zoe!" she shouted.

"Mommy. Hurry. The man's going to get me."

"Where is he, Zoe?" Stefan asked.

"He's grabbing at my feet."

Stefan shoved his gun away. "Start digging," he shouted.

Two rocks in and they were able to pull Zoe out. Water rushed from the hole.

Faith picked her up and rocked her. "Are you okay?"

Zoe nodded. "Catcher and me escaped the bad man. We got wet."

"I see that."

A man's arm stuck out of the hole. "Help," he gurgled against the churning water.

Stefan grabbed a large tree limb and dug away at the edges of the small hole. Water rushed out, and the man squirted through. He lay on the ground, gasping for air.

He looked over at Zoe and glared at her. "Kid, you ruined my life."

Zoe glared at him. "Then you shouldn't have been bad."

STEFAN STOOD OUTSIDE the room at the medical clinic in Trouble, Texas. Waiting. Daniel walked up to him and placed a hand on his shoulder. "Ransom called. They found Burke Thomas's body at the base of the cliff. He died on impact."

"It's for the best. Faith and Zoe have their lives back now." Stefan didn't think too hard about the emptiness lingering in his heart. He couldn't change reality. "What about the guy we brought in?"

"He's in custody. Singing like a canary. He worked for both Thomases. Cleaned up a lot of messes. He's added several names to Burke Thomas's kill list. Not to mention more than one politician who will be resigning. Starting with a couple of police commissioners who looked the other way."

"Good riddance." Stefan shot a glance at the closed door.

"How are they doing?" Daniel asked.

"Zoe's a tough kid. Faith's a tough woman. They'll get through this."

"So what are you doing out here?"

Stefan shook his head. "Nothing's changed. Faith has her life back. I never will. I need to rendezvous with Annie soon."

The thought depressed him. He didn't think he'd ever get over Faith and Zoe.

"I wouldn't be so sure about that." Ransom Grainger walked into the hallway.

Stefan quirked a brow. "I didn't expect to see you here."

"I'm here for a couple of reasons. First, I wanted to meet the woman who put together the research that would've nailed Burke Thomas if he hadn't taken a nose dive."

Stefan narrowed his gaze at his boss. "What are you thinking?"

"I can always use a good researcher in CTC. I'm planning to offer her a job."

"Like hell you are."

"What's it to you?" Ransom said. "You're taking off anyway. Besides, the pay's great. I don't think she'll turn me down."

Stefan glared at his boss. "I don't want her in danger. She needs a normal life. I don't know one member of CTC who has a normal life."

"I do," Daniel said.

"You quit," Stefan reminded him. "And I don't have a choice. You know that. The Thomases outed me. My cover's blown."

Ransom cleared his throat. "If you weren't in danger, would you stay?"

Stefan's jaw throbbed so hard it ached. "It's not a choice I have."

Ransom started to speak, but Stefan just shook his head. Before his boss could say anything, the hospital room opened.

"How's Zoe?" Stefan asked, placing his hands on Faith's arms.

Faith shook her head in bewilderment. "A few scrapes and bruises, but she's not even fazed. She thought the whole thing was a big adventure. And of course, she and Catcher have bonded."

Faith smiled at Daniel. "Thanks for coming."

He kissed her cheek. "I guess we know where that puppy's going. I'm glad you're both okay."

Faith frowned. "I haven't told her about her father yet. I don't know what to say."

"Tell her as much of the truth as you can. Over time, you can fill in the blanks," Daniel offered. "You'll know what she can handle."

She glanced at Stefan. "She wants to see you."

"Sure." Stefan followed Faith into Zoe's room.

"Stefan." Zoe smiled at him. "I like your new name best of all."

He winced at the bruises on her head and the scrapes on her arms. "How you doing, Slugger?"

"That's what my mom calls me."

"I know. But after you escaped from that bad guy, I've decided it's the perfect name for you."

She beamed at him. "Mommy, where's my backpack?"

"Here, sweetie. It's heavy."

"I know. That's what I wanted to show Stefan." She unzipped the front pouch and pulled out a large rock.

Stefan let out a low whistle. "Where'd you find that, Zoe?"

"In the cave. A bunch of rocks fell and there was this tunnel. A big stack of yellow rocks were just sitting there, piled up. I almost went down that tunnel, but the ceiling was coming down."

"You did the right thing. Can I hold it?" he asked.

"Sure." She shrugged. "I'm going to keep it in my collection."

Stefan weighed it in his hand. "Zoe, I think this is a very large chunk of gold. Real gold."

Faith gasped. "You're kidding."

Zoe took the stone from him. "It's worth a lot of money? Enough for me to buy Catcher? Please, Mom. Can I have him?"

Faith looked over at Stefan. "His bark led us to you. Of course you can keep him."

"Yay! I can't wait to show Daddy. He said I could keep Catcher at Grandma and Grandpa's house. Where is he?"

Faith cleared her throat. Stefan hurt at her struggle, but this was one thing he couldn't protect Zoe from. She sat on her daughter's bed. "Slugger, I have something to tell you."

Looking at her innocent face and open expression, Stefan tensed. He placed his hand on Faith's shoulder and squeezed. He felt a shudder run through her, and then she stilled.

"Zoe, your daddy was in an accident in the mountains. He got hurt. Really bad."

Zoe bowed her head. "Is he in the hospital?"

"No, honey." Faith pulled Zoe into her lap. "Zoe, your daddy is gone. He didn't make it off the mountain."

Zoe looked at her, eyes tearing up. "I won't ever see him again?"

Faith hugged her close. "I'm sorry, baby."

Zoe cried for several minutes. She bit her lip and looked over at Stefan. "Was my daddy a bad man?"

"What do you think, Zoe?" Stefan asked, his voice

quiet. He didn't want to lie to Zoe, but he didn't want her to hear the truth. Not yet.

"He gave me to that bad man. That wasn't nice."

"No, it wasn't." Stefan knelt down next to her. "My dad did some bad things, Zoe. But I still loved him. It's okay to still love him."

Tears fell down her cheeks and she leaned into Stefan. He wrapped his arms around her and rested his cheek on her hair. God, he was going to miss her.

He met Faith's gaze over Zoe's head. He was going to miss them both so much, his heart might never be the same.

FAITH'S HEART BROKE for Zoe. She rested her hand on Zoe's head as her daughter hugged Stefan. He cradled her daughter close. Tears welled behind Faith's eyes.

Stefan had kept his promise. He'd saved them both. She nestled next to them on the bed. They sat there for a few minutes, just being quiet. No words were necessary.

It was over.

Faith didn't know how long they sat there when a nurse entered the room with a wheelchair. "Miss Zoe. The doctor wants to do an X-ray of that arm."

Zoe lifted her head from Stefan's chest and bit her lip. "Will it hurt?"

"Not at all. You just have to lie there and he'll take a picture."

"I'll come with you," Faith offered.

"I have to be a big girl." Zoe lifted her chin. "I can do it by myself, Mom."

Faith didn't know what to say to that. She and her daughter were so alike. Faith wanted Zoe to grow into a self-sufficient young woman, but not so she wouldn't let herself accept help when she needed it.

She looked over at Stefan. He'd taught her that sometimes you could actually count on someone else to have your back.

Stefan ruffled Zoe's hair. "You don't have to do everything on your own, Zoe. We all need help sometimes."

"Not you."

"Even me. How about your mom and I come with you?"

"I can do it myself. I'm not scared."

Stefan raised his brow. "What if we want to be with you because we missed you?"

Zoe let out a long sigh. "I guess that's okay."

The nurse chuckled, but Faith caught a bit of relief in her daughter's eyes.

Zoe winced as she got out of bed. The large bruise showing from the sleeve of her hospital gown had grown even darker purple.

"That arm looks like it hurts, Slugger."

"It's okay, Mommy. The water shoved me into the rocks. Or it coulda been when I fell in the hole. Lots of stuff happened in that cave."

"You've got a tough daughter," the nurse said.

"I know." Faith smiled down at Zoe. "She's the best."

The nurse wheeled Zoe out of the room. Faith and Stefan followed.

"Well, it's clear both of you love her very much,"

the nurse said. "I may be old-fashioned, but that's always the best medicine."

Faith's gaze flew to Stefan's. Did they really look like a family?

When they reached the X-ray room door, the nurse stopped them. She wheeled Zoe inside. When the door closed, Faith sighed. "Is she handling all this too well?"

"I don't know. She's something else, that's for sure."

Faith sat down, and Stefan moved a chair around to face her. He took her hands in his. "Look, I don't know how much longer I can stay. The men who want to kill me will start coming. You and Zoe need to be safe. I couldn't live with myself if anything happened to you."

"You're leaving? Now?"

"I have to. I don't have a choice, Faith."

She bit down on her lip. "You know, I've just realized my daughter is braver than I am." She met his gaze. "So I'm just going to ask. If things were different, would you want to stay with us?"

Stefan touched her cheek gently. "Oh, yeah. You and Zoe brought me back to life, Faith. I was dead inside before you came into my world."

She took in a shallow breath. "Then take us with you. Nothing is stopping you."

He shook his head. "I can't let you give up everything. It's not fair to you. Or to Zoe. She needs a future, not a life on the run."

Faith couldn't stop the tears from rolling down her cheeks. "I love you, Stefan."

She held her breath. He closed his eyes, then opened them. "I love you, too. More than you'll ever know.

That's why I can't let you come with me, Faith. You and Zoe deserve a normal life. A happy life."

"Zoe and I deserve to be loved. And that's you." She grabbed his hand and held it to her heart. "I've never met a man who was willing to drop everything just to help two strangers. You saw we were in trouble and didn't take no for an answer. Why won't you accept the same from me?"

Stefan groaned, rose from the chair and pulled her close. His body trembled against hers. She couldn't believe she made him shake with longing.

He kissed her eyelids, her cheeks and finally her lips before holding her against him. "I shouldn't. It won't be fair to you."

"Leaving us isn't fair, either."

The nurse wheeled the chair back out. Zoe looked from her mom back to Stefan. She smiled. "I like you like that."

"We'll take her back to her room," he said as he cleared his throat, his voice rough with emotion.

"The doctor will be up soon to give you the results," the nurse said.

Stefan wheeled Zoe down the hall while Faith walked beside her.

"Slugger," Faith asked. "What would you think if we went with Stefan when he leaves here?"

She frowned. "Could we take Catcher?"

"Of course."

"And you'd be there, too?"

"Yes."

"Forever?"

"Absolutely."

Zoe grinned. "I like that idea. He makes your eyes smile, Mom. And you always look happy."

Stefan knelt down in front of her. "Zoe, there's a catch. If you come with me, we can't see our friends again. We'll start a new life."

"But you'll be there? You promise? You'll take care of Mom so she's not alone and sad anymore?"

Stefan met Faith's gaze. "I'll take care of both of you. I promise."

Zoe grinned. "Okay. We can do that. As long as we have a backyard."

Epilogue

The crisp air on the Triple C Ranch was soaked with a hint of pine and cinnamon. Christmas had its own special aroma. Stefan hadn't thought about such things in, well, ever, but Zoe had brought the fact out to him, so...

He paced back and forth in the small room where he waited.

A soft knock sounded at the door and his best man walked in. Daniel Adams grinned. "I've seen you waiting to infiltrate a terrorist organization and be less nervous than this."

Stefan frowned. "After five months hiding out, testifying against Orren, and learning how many women Burke brutalized over the years, Ransom's got our second set of new identities ready, but this time it'll be permanent. No going back. I just don't know if Faith and Zoe really understand what this change will mean. Zoe will miss her grandmother. The poor woman lost her family and had no idea what was going on. The truth is, I don't know if I'm doing the right thing taking them away from everything they know."

Daniel shook his head. "How about you trust your soon-to-be wife to make that decision?"

"She loves me," Stefan said, still unnerved by that fact. "She wants to be with me wherever I am."

"Definitely a crazy woman who doesn't know what she's talking about," Daniel said with a smile. "And what about you? Can you imagine your life without her?"

Just the words made Stefan's heart twist. "She brought me back to life."

"Then quit worrying. I'll tell you from experience, whatever your name is, wherever your life, it won't be perfect, but it'll be an adventure."

Daniel left the room, but Stefan couldn't let the doubts recede. He had to give her one more chance. One more opportunity to come to her senses, even if she shattered his heart in the process. He loved her too much not to give her the chance to live a normal life.

He peeked out into the foyer of CTC's headquarters. He heard a lot of voices. The house was filled with his friends and coworkers. Surprising how many he'd made over the years.

Faith was just down the hall getting help from Mrs. Hargraves, Raven and a couple other CTC wives.

He walked quietly down the hallway and tapped lightly on the door.

"Come in," Faith said.

He walked inside and his breath stopped.

She stood before him, shoulders bare, lace hugging her body and flowing to the floor in a pool of iridescence. She was his dream. He swallowed and the sound seemed to echo through the room.

Her eyes grew wide, frantic. "What are you doing here?"

"I have no idea," he said. "You are…more than beautiful."

She flushed, pink lacing her cheeks. "Thank you. Burke…uh, Burke picked out a poofy, pastry-shaped monstrosity. Marrying you. This is *my* fairy tale."

Stefan knew he should walk away, but he couldn't. He took her hands in his. "Last chance for a normal life."

She tilted her head. "I have no doubts." She frowned at his transparent expression. "Do you?"

"Every moment of every day. I want you and Zoe to be happy. What if we have to move during the middle of baseball season?"

"Then we'll survive. As long as we're together. Whatever else happens, we'll take as it comes."

He leaned down and kissed her lips, feeling the warmth under his mouth. "I have something for you," he whispered.

"We can't." She grinned. "Not before the wedding."

He reached into his pocket and pulled out a small velvet pouch. "I found this for you. I wanted you to have it back." He tilted the fabric and a small silver ring dropped into his hand. The traditional wedding ring had two small diamonds on either side of a modest square-cut.

Faith gasped. "It can't be. I pawned Mama's ring."

Her gaze flew to his. "How could you have possibly found it?"

"It took a little searching, and a little bit of digging where you'd been from Zoe."

Her hands trembled as she slipped the ring on her right hand. "Thank you, Stefan. I can't—"

"You don't have to say anything. I'd do anything for you and Zoe."

"I never had a doubt." She straightened. "So, are you going to marry me and then disappear into the ether? I'm ready if you are."

"Well, I'm not."

Stefan whirled around. He couldn't believe who was standing there in the doorway, looking every inch a royal. "Kat?"

Queen Katherine of Bellevaux grinned and raced across the room to hug him tight. "Did you think I was going to let my big brother get married without the family?"

Two six-year-olds ran across the room. "Hi, Uncle Stefan. 'Member me? I'm Hayden."

"I'm Lanie," a precious little blond-haired girl said, hugging his leg. "Mama told us all about you. You're a hero." She looked up at Faith. "You're dressed like a fairy princess." She straightened. "Did you know I'm a princess, too?"

Stefan froze. "What are you doing here? It's not safe."

"Don't worry... Stefan," Logan Carmichael said as he stepped into the room, holding a year-old cutie pie in his arms. The man who'd married his sister, who'd become Prince Consort of Bellevaux.

"I don't understand."

Ransom Grainger walked in.

"Well, everyone, just come on in," Stefan said.

Logan handed his daughter to his wife. "The last few years we've been working to break up the group who put the hit out on you. We captured Chanteaux last week. There's nobody left who wants you dead, Stefan. You can come home."

He staggered back. "Home?" He looked at Faith. She appeared to be in a state of shock. He definitely was.

"But—"

"I'll step aside, Stefan. Logan and I have discussed it. The throne is yours if you want it."

Stefan's mind whirled with shock. *Throne.*

"No, Katherine. Our people have embraced you and Logan. You've already done so much good. Besides, I never wanted to be king. If I have to legally abdicate, I will, but I want a normal life." He kissed Faith's hand. "With the woman I love."

"You're still a prince," Kat reminded him.

"What's going on?" a voice demanded. Zoe stood there, dressed in a tuxedo, not a hint of lace anywhere. A large reddish dog hovered by her side.

Stefan knelt down. "Zoe, how would you like to be a princess?"

She looked at him like he was crazy. "No, thanks. I like baseball better."

"Me, too." Stefan laughed. "Thanks for the offer,

Kat, but you can keep the throne. I've already found my dream come true."

He pulled Faith into his arms. "My fairy tale began the moment I met you."

"A normal life," she said softly. "Are you ready for that?"

Stefan smiled down at her. "With you and Zoe in my life, it will always be an adventure."

* * * * *

Franklin County, Tennessee
Monday, February 25, 9:10 p.m.

The red-and-blue lights flashed in the night.

Audrey Anderson opened her car door and stepped out
onto the gravel road. She grimaced and wished she'd taken
time to change her shoes, but time was not an available luxury
when the police scanner spit out the code for a shooting that
ended in a call to the coroner. Good thing her dedicated editor,
Brian Peterson, had his ear to the police radio pretty much
24/7 and immediately texted her.

The sheriff's truck was already on-site, along with two
county cruisers and the coroner's van. So far no news vans
and no cars that she noticed belonging to other reporters
from the tri-county area. Strange, that cocky reporter from
the *Tullahoma Telegraph* almost always arrived on the scene
before Audrey. Maybe she had a friend in the department.

Then again, Audrey had her own sources, too. She reached
back into the car for her bag. So far the closest private source
she had was the sheriff himself—which was only because he
still felt guilty for cheating on her back in high school.

Audrey was not above using that guilt whenever the need
arose.

Tonight seemed like the perfect time to remind the man she'd once thought she would marry that he owed her one or two or a hundred.

She shuddered as the cold night air sent a shiver through her. Late February was marked by all sorts of lovely blooms and promises of spring, but it was all just an illusion. It was still winter and Mother Nature loved letting folks know who was boss. Like tonight—the gorgeous sixty-two-degree sunny day had turned into a bone-chilling evening. Audrey shivered, wishing she'd worn a coat to dinner.

Buncombe Road snaked through a farming community situated about halfway between Huntland and Winchester—every agricultural mile fell under the Franklin County sheriff's jurisdiction. The houses, mostly farmhouses sitting amid dozens if not hundreds of acres of pastures and fields, were scattered few and far between. But that wasn't the surprising part of the location. This particular house and farm belonged to a Mennonite family. Rarely did violence or any other sort of trouble within this quiet, closed community ripple beyond its boundaries. Most issues were handled privately and silently. The Mennonites kept to themselves for the most part and never bothered anyone. A few operated public businesses within the local community, and most interactions were kept strictly within the business domain. There was no real intermingling or socializing within the larger community—not even Winchester, which was the county seat and buzzed with activity.

Whatever happened inside this turn-of-the-nineteenth-century farmhouse tonight was beyond the closed community's ability to settle amid their own ranks.

Don't miss
In Self Defense *by Debra Webb,*
available February 2019 wherever
Harlequin® Intrigue *books and ebooks are sold.*

www.Harlequin.com